Breaking

Boundaries

Breaking Boundaries

An Anthology of Horror and Dark Science Fiction

Gayl J. Spear, editor

21-SPEA

Library of Congress Number: 2001119384
ISBN #:   Hardcover   1-4010-3574-4
            Softcover   1-4010-3573-6

www.breakingboundariesbook.com

These are works of fiction. Names, characters, places, and incidents are products of the authors' imaginations, or are fictionalized for dramatic purposes and are not to be construed as real. Any resemblance to actual events, locales, organizations, or persons living or dead is purely coincidental.

And kind of creepy, wouldn't you say?

This book was printed in the United States of America.

To order additional copies of this book, contact:
Xlibris Corporation
1-888-7-XLIBRIS
www.Xlibris.com
Orders@Xlibris.com

*Dedicated to the writers and editors who have spent their lives,
their talents, and their souls in service of their craft.*

Contents

Welcome to the dark

Visit:
a future in which memories are no longer your own
a world in which humans are chattel for a grotesque new
species

Witness:
a lawyer contending with the forces of Hell itself
a spirit crying out for justice to a most unlikely savior

Feel:
your own mind slip away as you regress into madness
the last, desperate charge of heroism against the endless night

Borders, like rules, were meant to be broken.

Welcome to *Breaking Boundaries*

Why Breaking Boundaries?

by Gayl J. Spear

In the summer of 2000 (you remember it—that was the year
that the computers all went haywire, the power grids collapsed,
and the subsequent riots and devastation cast society back into
the quasi-Dark Ages state it is now in), I finally reached the
point in my career where I'd had enough. Enough of editing what
other people told me to edit; enough of putting out books and
journals I didn't believe in.

Now, God knows that the last thing the world needs is another anthology, but that's what I decided, in the summer of 2000,
to put my efforts towards. Why?

Well, quite simply because so many anthologies already ex-
tant don't seem to pay attention to the writers who haven't yet
"made it." I've plunged headlong into innumerable "Best of . . ."
and "Year's Best . . ." and so on and so forth, only to find that, in
many cases, my reaction was, "Aren't these the same guys who
were the best *last* year?" As editors begin to writer and writers
begin to edit (and the two also have a relationship going back
years, if not decades), the chances of any honest-to-God "new
voices" being heard are slim to none.

So when I sat down to plan out what eventually became *Breaking Boundaries*, I determined that I would only publish the stories

I actually believed in, the stories that, to me, deserved to be in the anthology, based on my own, admittedly biased, criteria.

I also chose not to limit the book with a theme. I was tempted, I confess, especially when the first few entries came in and had absolutely no common thread, but I stuck to my guns. The only thing I asked potential contributors to do was "break a boundary."

And they did. In spades.

Some broke boundaries of form, as in Liam Grey's "Common Cold." Others broke boundaries of expectations, as in Scott Braden's "Sterling Silver." Still others broke boundaries of convention, of ethics, of tradition. In the case of author John Barrow and his "A New Ripper," every possible last boundary of good taste and propriety was not just broken, but trampled on and ground to dust.

Why "an anthology of horror and dark science fiction?" I've always loved speculative fiction. Even when growing up, when I was supposed to be interested in Barbie dolls or Betty Crocker Easy Bake Ovens, I always thought my brothers' *Star Wars* toys were far more interesting. I guess it is to them that I owe my abiding love for science fiction and horror—they were the ones who sneaked me into many a showing of *Close Encounters of the Third Kind* and kept me up late at night to watch the horror revivals on channel 13 in Baltimore.

Do horror and science-fiction belong together? I say, emphatically, yes. In fact, sometimes you can't tell the difference between the two. The book that definitively awakened me to the potential of fiction was Stephen King's *Carrie*. Like Carrie White, I was a somewhat shy teenager, and I could identify with her struggle . . . even as there were days when I desperately wished for her dark powers.

But do those powers belong to the province of horror or science-fiction? What about the little girl in *Firestarter*? What about author Kay Kenyon's *Leap Point*—undeniably science fiction, but horrifying enough that I couldn't sleep the night I finished reading it. What about Luke Skywalker's harrowing test in "the tree" in *The Empire Strikes Back*? (What about Jar-Jar Binks? Now *there's* horror for you!)

The two genres have always been interconnected in my mind. As Bonnie Hammer (of the Sci-Fi Channel) once said, "Horror is a part of science fiction. It belongs in the definition of sci-fi."

So. Throw all of these feelings, notions, and memories into a stew. Stir in ten generous dollops of the creepy, the radical, the monstrous, and the outright profane. Put it in the bright orange Betty Crocker Easy Bake Oven of your mind, and crank that little light bulb all the way up.

Something strange and wonderful is baking, and it's going to overflow the baking pan and break *all* the boundaries.

Unforget

by Barry Lyga

Barry Lyga has written everything from comic books to academic papers with titles like "Transparent Eyeballs and Similar Dismemberments." His short stories have been published in The Florida Review *and the* Calhoun Literary Arts Magazine, *and have also taken prizes in the Random House Book Fair contests.*

He is the author of the upcoming novels Blueblade *and* Founding Father, *as well as the co-screenwriter and producer of the upcoming short film* The Intensely Stupid Adventures of Norman Otto, *which is based on his limited-run comic strip of the same name.*

Barry lives in the wilds of Maryland, under the watchful eyes of his wife and a vicious three-pound dwarf rabbit.

Unforget

*W*hen *I was twelve years old, my Uncle Henry took me down to the basement, pulled my pants down, and fellated me to my first orgasm. I can still remember the smell of engine grease from the lawn mower, which my dad stored in the basement during the winter—a dull, dark odor. I think of it and I remember how he turned me around and bent me over and—*

No, wait. That wasn't me. That was someone else. Kyle Landingham. Case #1758-PK/9.

Damn. Damn.

I walked into the precinct after a week's vacation at one of the Moon's private resorts, where you can forget about Earth, since it's always on the other side. There's an old song from almost a hundred years ago that I always think of when I go there. Something like "See you on the dark side of the moon." That's all I can remember.

Or actually, that's all Linda DaVont could remember. She was a 120-year-old widow we found strangled to death outside her own home a few years ago. I got the guy who killed her for nothing more than the computer on her wrist and the creds in her purse. I also got a brainful of twen-cen trivia in the bargain.

I ducked into the bathroom before heading to the E.D. offices. Sometimes it helps to look at yourself in the mirror, just in case you forget what you look like. It happens—not often, but it does, and I'm the sort of guy who believes in preventative maintenance. They made a movie about guys like me once. In the movie, the main character forgets his own identity, and there's a scene where he's staring into a mirror, crying because he doesn't recognize . . .

I cleared my throat and took inventory: Crooked nose that had been broken a couple of times, but didn't look too out of place on my angular face. Shoulder-length brown hair, with eyes the color of milk chocolate. My skin was bleached like snow from a week of moonbathing and high-rad force fields. The bathroom started to creep me out. Once, many years ago, a stranger grabbed me from behind while I was in a lavatory just like this one. He pulled me down to my knees by my hair and made me—

No. No. That was Eleanor Pulaski.

I splashed some water on my face, checked myself again, then headed into the Engram Division.

The office hadn't changed at all since I'd last been in. Cops sat in scattered privacy fields, dictating reports to their PDAs or catching up on computer work. My wireless wrist unit plugged into the Division database as soon as I entered the room and fed me an update.

I went into Captain Gresard's office. He was a squat, florid-faced man with a skull like a topographic map, hairless and bulging with veins. "You should cut your fucking hair," he told me before I could even speak.

"Good to see you, too, Cap." I replied, and dropped into a chair across from his desk. "Need me to handle the new case?"

"And your sideburns are a goddamned disgrace," he went on. He jammed a smokeless cigarette into his mouth and sucked. When he inhaled, his face got even redder, and his veins twitched. "You think you're working vice or something?

"The new case is a rape," he told me, after leeching some more synthetic endorphins from the cigarette. "You take this, I don't want any of that shit like with the serial rapist last year. I *should* give it to Chapman."

I bristled, remembering. "That was last year. I was in a bad place, Cap. I'm better now. Besides, Chapman's a woman. You give her another rape case this year, she'll be skirting on the edge of neurotic burn. And besides, the shrinks have given me a clean bill of—"

He snorted laughter through his nose, a clear indication of the esteem in which he held the Division's shrinks. "Get out of here," he growled, "and shave, for Christ's sake." His endearing way of giving me the case.

I almost bumped into Chapman herself as I left the Captain's office. She was a petite brunette, with enormous green eyes that surely must have glowed in the dark. She reminded me of my sister, Kathleen.

Kathleen, who died six years ago, shot dead by a skyjacker who wanted her floater. I was sitting in the passenger seat when it happened, and all I could do was watch as he pulled the trigger.

No. Wait a minute. I never had a sister. Mark de la Vox had a sister named Kathleen. I caught the skyjacker and saw the guy convicted. Case #0875-PK/6.

I blinked back the memory, so clear and so powerful. Kathleen's head jerking, spastic in the grip of an electric bullet . . .

"Paul?" Chapman asked. "You okay?"

"Sure," I lied, grinning. "Just . . ."

"Remembering something," she finished knowingly. "You going to take the rape?"

"Yeah."

"I'm awful sorry about that." She sounded genuinely apologetic. "I should have taken it for you, but regs . . ."

"Don't worry about it." I put a hand on her shoulder. Based on our psych profiles, there were limits to which cases we could all take and when, to prevent neurotic burn. "You'll probably get a messy murder or mutilation."

She laughed shortly. "Lucky me, right?"

I waggled a hand at her in farewell and headed out the door.

My wrist unit had already grabbed the case file from the infracomputer system: Now logged as Case #2897-PK/6. Heather Martagna. Rape in the first degree.

I went to my car.

I guess it all started about fifty years ago, when the first fruits of the Human Genome Project were borne. That was when the neurologists finally got their hands on the amino acid sequences that allowed them to manipulate the hippocampus, the part of the brain that controls memory construction. They could tease engrams into shape, leading to a whole new science based on neurogenesis. In the med journals, they started referring to the process as "engrammar."

At first, it was used to help people with memory loss and severe brain damage. But then the depression of '51 hit and you had something like 75% of the population working part-time. Which meant that they had a lot of time on their hands, and not a lot of money. Put those two factors together and you'd've had a massive upswing in the crime rate even if the NRA coalition in Congress hadn't started its free gun giveaway program as a way of getting around the gun-seller background checks. "Just because it's the Second Amendment doesn't mean it's second in importance," read their campaign literature.

Crime got so bad that soon statistics showed that almost everyone knew someone who had been the victim of a violent crime. The cops and the courts were outgunned, overwhelmed, and understaffed. That was when someone got the bright idea to combine neurogenesis and police work.

At first, they called them "Revenge Cops." The prevailing thought was that if you downloaded a crime victim's memory and uploaded it into a cop's hippocampus, the cop would actually be able to remember the crime himself. Not only would he be able to get details that the victim might not be able to describe accurately, but he'd also have a personal recollection of the event . . . and a personal reason to bring the criminal to justice.

I guess they were a little surprised at first. Like most science, engrammar turned out to be an art. Some cops went off the deep end, relentless in their pursuit. Others went psychotic, unable to handle the schism of memories that weren't really their own, but felt real.

And so the Engram Division was formed, made up of guys like me, who were subjected to exhaustive batteries of tests before being allowed to take our first upload. Not all crimes are referred to us—just the ones where all other alternatives have been exhausted . . . or where the victim demands it.

Which is what Heather Martagna had done.

I pulled up at her house just as the sun was setting overhead. It seemed dull and blurry, Earthside. But huge. From the Moon, it's a hard, bright disc.

She had a little brownstone on one of those city boulevards with trees and uncracked sidewalks. You know the kind I'm talking about—those parts of the city that don't look like they're in the city.

I flashed her my badge data through the door port, and she opened up once her house system decrypted the info and pronounced it good. Like most recent rape victims, she was wary, angry, and terrified all at once. A young, pretty blonde woman desperately trying not to look young or pretty or even blonde, her body a black mass of oversized sweatshirt, her hair tucked unevenly under a baseball cap. One cheek was blemished with still-healing abrasions.

"Miss Martagna?" I said gently. "Can I come in?"

She nodded slowly and backed up. I resisted the urge to shut the door behind me, letting her do it instead. Let her retain control of the environment.

We stood in the vestibule for a moment. "Is there somewhere we can talk?" I asked.

She blinked and for an instant, I saw her true face, the one she'd worn until her assault two weeks ago, the one she would wear again. Someday.

"Of course. God, I'm sorry. I'm so sorry . . ." She trailed off as she led me into a small but well-appointed living room. I took the seat she offered and watched as she curled up in a corner of the sofa, pulling her legs beneath her and tucking the end of her sweatshirt between them.

"My name is Paul Kalladaf," I told her, then grinned when I saw the puzzlement on her face. "It's English and Arabic. One of those new-breed surnames that were popular back at the Turn of the Century."

She relaxed a little bit. They usually did.

"Are you sure you understand the procedure? This isn't something you should enter into lightly."

She shrugged her shoulders. "The other officers, the ones who took my statement? They explained it to me. They told me that, given the nature of my . . . case . . ."—she struggled with the word, clearly preferring to use another—". . . that this would give the best results."

"That's true. I've already looked at their notes and the doctor's report. There's not much there."

"It's not my fault!" she burst out. "I can't—"

Without thinking, I got up and went to her, putting my arms around her. Traditional police work frowns on such contact, but in my field, it's encouraged. After all, we would soon be so much more intimate.

She pushed me away and pressed herself deeper into the sofa, like a turtle retreating into its shell. I chided myself inwardly for moving too quickly.

"No one's blaming you," I told her. "Some cases shake out this way, that's all."

She sniffled back tears. "I understand. I'm sorry for losing control like that."

I let her go, but stayed on the sofa with her. "That's perfectly understandable. I want to make certain that you understand what you're getting into, though."

Confusion clouded her eyes. "I thought it was just a simple procedure—"

"The procedure is very simple. The aftermath may not be. I'll have your complete memory of the attack, Heather. Right down to what you were thinking and feeling. Do you understand?"

She nodded.

"Now, this means that I can do a better job looking for the man who raped you. It means that when he goes to trial, I can testify for you so that you don't have to face him in court."

"So what's so bad?" she asked.

"Well, for one thing, I'll have that memory forever. Even when the day comes that you recover from this, someone will still be walking around with that memory. Can you handle knowing that?"

She watched me for long moments. The eager ones I worry about. The ones who blow off my concern. But she turned the idea over in her head a couple times, looking at it from all the angles.

"That's fine," she whispered.

"But there's more. Do you know what an engram is?"

"I think so."

"To think of it in physical terms, an engram is a discrete 'chunk' of memory. It's what makes up your memories. That's what will be copied from you to me through the synthetic neurogenesis process. But what you need to understand is that memories *aren't* physical things. Sometimes you can't tell where one starts and the other ends. Do you follow? Sometimes related memories—or even unrelated ones—can get caught up in an engram. Pieces of things, stuck in a memory like pebbles in mortar."

"So you might get things from me that aren't related to my . . . case?"

"Exactly. If something about him—maybe his aftershave, maybe his hands—reminded you of an old boyfriend, I might pick up some memories of that boyfriend. Memories that you don't *want* me to have, but I'll have them anyway. Maybe you had a rape fantasy once upon a time—" She turned away angrily.

"Heather, many women fantasize about it. That doesn't mean you caused it or liked it. But if you did, I might get that fantasy, too. Do you see what I mean? It can be anything. That's also why they can't just remove the memory later—it might become associated with my own memories, and I could risk losing—"

She faced me again, and tears were streaming down her face. "I just want you to catch him. Whatever it takes." She looked at me with haunted eyes. "Because until you do, I won't be able to sleep."

The next day, she came down to the Engram Division. With a living person whose precipitating event is relatively recent, the process is pretty simple. It's not like people who have suppressed the memory for years, or with fresh corpses, where the process can take hours over several days and involve as many misses as hits. With someone like Heather Martagna, it's easy.

She laid down in the scan tube and accepted the sleep meds. Once she was out, the doctors sent a fiber optic probe into her brain, passing it between her eyeball and her eye socket. The little probe headed straight for the hippocampus, using a carefully coded sequence of amino acids to attract the right engram.

Once the doctors were certain they'd located the memory, they fed in a second probe through the other eye. This one did a complete scan of the engram, recording its nucleotide arrangement down to the nanoscopic level.

Then it was my turn.

I don't even need the sleep meds any more. I have a tiny, undetectable chute in the corner of my left eye, like almost every other ED cop I can think of. The doctors took the information from the second probe and programmed a third probe with it.

Then I went ahead and slid the third probe into my own brain. Just like putting in an earring, only with less discomfort. There are no nerves that transmit pain in the brain, after all.

The third probe used my body's own hippocampus and memory apparatus to re-assemble the memory it had grabbed from Heather, rebuilding the whole engram molecule by molecule. By the time Heather had woken up and rubbed sleep out of her eyes, I had downloaded her rape straight into my hippocampus.

It would take some time and the proper stimulus for me actually to remember the rape, just as it would with any memory of my own. Something would have to jog my memory. Usually, I spoke to the victim after the download and used their recollection to jump-start my own, but Heather had an allergic reaction to the sleep meds and had to go home.

So I sat in my privacy field and flipped through the digital note screens of the cops who had originally interviewed Heather Martagna. "Victim was walking home from a friend's house . . ." I started to get some flickers—

—". . . heard a sound behind her, but thought it was a cat she had just walked past . . ."—

—some flickers of something—

—". . . noticed a shadow cast by a nearby streetlight . . ."—

—*tabby cat, all fat and puffy looking, its head jerking up, startled, as I walk by, God my calves are killing me why did I wear the heels*—

—". . . began to walk faster, and noticed that the person behind her was moving more quickly, as well . . ."—

—*could that be? Could that be someone walking after me? Did I bring a stun capsule? Can I get into my purse in time?*—

—flickers, coming faster and stronger, God, my heart rate accelerating—

—*shit, he's got me now, I can't believe this, kick back at him, stumble, oh stupid, stupid heels, can't get my balance, he's pushing me down, scream you dumb bitch! What's wrong with me? Scream for help but I can't the wind's knocked out me, my ankle hurts what did I do to it stupid heels why did I wear the heels?*

Try to turn around. See him. See him. But he steps on my hand—Goddamnit!—and I suck in air with the pain, sprawled on my stomach, his hands on my ankles—

"—while Ms. Martagna was still stunned, the perpetrator pulled her bodily into a nearby abandoned building. Statement supported by abrasions cited in medical report and damage to clothes, invoiced as—"

—tearing my blouse, my bra—

And he forces my face against the floor, the concrete cold and rough against my cheek, and then flipping up my skirt and

And when it's over, he pushes me roughly aside, then disappears, nothing more than footfalls fading into the distance, percussion to my sobs.

"Paul?" Someone was standing in front of me. She said the name again. "Paul, snap out of it. You're having a neurotic episode."

A pretty woman, with brown hair and green eyes. She should wear different make-up. She'd be prettier. She'd—

"Paul! Listen to me." Why was she calling me Paul? Why?

"Your name is Paul Kalladaf. You're an Engram Division detective."

"No," I told her, my voice sounding strangely deep. "My name is Heather—"

And then the woman grabbed me between the legs. I gasped. I had a penis! What the hell—

I blinked and recognized Chapman standing before me. I had drifted too far into Heather's memories, and Chapman had come by to shake me out of the neurotic state. "I'm all right, Chapman." She regarded me with suspicion.

"I'm okay," I assured her. "Mind letting go?"

She blushed and released my privates. "Sorry."

"That's okay. Thanks for stopping by." I tried to stand, found myself wobbly. I leaned against Chapman.

"Take it easy," she said. "Your sense of balance is thrown. You don't have breasts and your hips aren't—"

"I know," I told her. It took a moment, but soon I got used to my own body again. Cross-gender memory transfer always has its side effects. More than a few cops have had gender reassignment after living in the mind of the opposite sex. Chapman herself once got drunk at a party and confided to me that she tends to think of herself as a man. "Sometimes," she told me, slurring, "at night, when I wake up, I forget and end up pissing all over my legs when I try to pee standing up."

I could still feel Heather Martagna's pain, her anguish, her humiliation. The rape detectives' note screen was still flashing, so I switched it off.

"Recent assault, right?" Chapman asked.

I nodded and took my seat again. "Yeah. The memory's extremely vivid." I shifted uncomfortably. I'd handled rapes before, and every time, I go through a period of time where I'm uneasy with my own equipment. I had just experienced a penis used a weapon, and the idea of one hanging between my legs was almost nauseating.

"Any clues? Anything helpful?"

I frowned. "I don't think she ever saw him. He came up to her from behind, raped her from behind, kept her face down at all times . . ."

"Sounds? Voice? Smells?" She was trying to help, but there was nothing for it. I was disoriented and nothing was clicking.

"Bigger than my last boyfriend," I mumbled.

"What?"

"Christ, I'm getting all kinds of subconscious stuff. He was bigger than her last boyfriend. Some part of her noticed that."

Chapman sighed. "Go home and get some sleep. That usually helps me. Sometimes the stuff comes up in your dreams. Or their dreams."

I let her help me up and checked out of the shift. Back at my apartment, I felt a moment of sudden and complete terror as I entered the living room. He was here. I was convinced of it. He had followed me, followed me back to my house . . .

No. I shook my head. That was part of Heather's engram, her fear of her attacker's return. But I locked my door, encrypted the software bolt with a gigabyte key, and drew my revolver. I checked behind the curtains and the sofa, peeked into all the corners and dark nooks in my apartment. He *could* be here. Uncle Henry could be here, ready to skyjack—

Damn. Bleed-through. Engrams colliding. The brain makes connections all its own, and I was dredging up all my synthetic neurogenetic implants based on the common threads of trauma and anger. I was losing focus.

The room lit up as lightning silently flickered outside. A moment later, a crashing bolt of thunder erupted, nearly driving my ears into my skull. The windows pattered with rain, then built to an endless throbbing as the wind buffeted drops against the plexiglass. I spent a few moments worrying about my cat—I didn't see it in the apartment, so it must have gone outside through the pet door—and then realized that I had never owned a cat. Landingham had, I think. Maybe Heather did, for all I knew.

My mind was reeling. I couldn't focus. I needed help concentrating, but the bleed-through and the rain were shredding my brain.

I put my gun on the end table and sat down, fishing in my inner coat pocket for my snuff box. I unlatched the lid, took a pinch of the lemon-scented powder between my fingers and snorted it. Even in the twen-cen, scientists knew that the smell of lemon stimulated the hippocampus.

The first snort helped clear my head a little bit. I took another one and I was back in the abandoned building, shaking in fear and shock while I was raped by a man whose face I never saw.

When he's finished, I feel him withdraw quickly, and some part of me, some stupid, cold, note taking part of me, thinks that he's bigger than my last boyfriend. And I feel what he's left running out of me, and I think I could get pregnant, I have to get an afterday from a doctor, and then I think "Is he going to kill me?" but already his steps are receding.

The sound of his feet. Further away. Other than a few grunts, the only noises he leaves me with.

I stay still for God knows how long, until I realize that I'm tearing up my face on the floor, that my backside is still in the air. I collapse onto the floor, then force myself to get up. He could come back. He could come back.

What if he knows where I live?

What if

What if

I don't know how long I relived it; I didn't look at the time. At some point, another blast of thunder roused me from Heather's memories, and I came back into the present, to find myself curled on the floor in a fetal position, my hands cupped protectively between my legs.

I rose on legs that felt like wet ropes. I didn't trust my hands on the controls of my car, so I commed a cab from my wrist unit. No more than twenty minutes later, I stood outside her brownstone, my overcoat collar turned up against the elements as the sky pelted me with water, rain sluicing down like a waterfall.

"I'm sorry for coming," I told her when she opened the door. "I'm really sorry—"

She let me in, and soon we were back in her living room. This time she put both of us on the sofa.

"I'm sorry," I said again. "Sorry to wake you up."

"I wasn't asleep. I was upstairs with the lights on and one of those little free guns you get when you open a bank account."

She laughed self-consciously. "I feel like a little girl, jumping at shadows and the rain and the thunder, but he—"

"He could be in the house," I finished. "That's what you're afraid of. He could be in the house."

Her throat worked silently and then she nodded, just once, as if ashamed to admit it.

"You lock the doors, check them all twice, maybe three times. You don't turn out the lights when you leave a room."

Another reluctant nod. "What if—"

"—he's still around? What if he knows where you live?"

Her head bobbed up and down. She couldn't believe it. It was like I was reading her mind. "What if he's—" she started.

"—an old boyfriend. Or a coworker. Someone who knows you. Someone who's been stalking you. He could be watching right now. He could come back and do it again."

She burst into tears, and I did so at the same time, our fear identical. We clutched each other, weeping. This time, she didn't push me away. This time she held onto me like I was an oxygen line and she a spacewalker.

"He was," she gasped between sobs, "he was bigger—"

"—than my last boyfriend," I finished.

"Such a stupid thing to remember," she said, her face against my shoulder. "Stupid. Stupid. I should have fought him. Why didn't I fight him? I was wearing—"

"—spiked heels."

"I could have kicked back, kicked him in the groin . . ."

"*Should* have. Why didn't I?"

"Fear, just paralyzed—"

"Like watching it happen to someone else, almost. And being unable to move . . ."

She pulled back and looked up at me in utter amazement. "That's *exactly* what it was like. *Exactly*. No one else has understood." Hushed awe. "Not my family, not my friends. They're all so damn sympathetic, but none of them—"

"None of them understand what happened to me," I said.

We stared at each other for what could have been an eternity or just a few seconds. "What happened to *you*, I mean."

She trembled. "God, now it's happened to you, too, right? Is this what I've done? Now I've raped you. Because of me, you feel it, too—"

I shook my head. "This is my job. This is what I do."

"Is it always so bad?" She touched my cheek gently, stroking away tears. "Is it always so hard?"

"It depends. Rapes . . . rapes are particularly hard. There was a guy last year . . . A serial rapist. We couldn't get anything on him. I had a few of his victims in my head, and there were just no clues. No evidence. It turns out he was using a rape stick. You know what a rape stick is?"

She shook her head.

"It's an illegally-amped VR set: a dildo with data implants, connected by microwave to a data-condom. He was using it on women, getting all the feedback, without even taking his pants off."

"Oh, God." She looked like she was going to throw up. I knew the feeling. I remembered my own revulsion so goddamned well.

"I caught him. I went a little nuts, I think. All those memories . . ."

"What," she asked hesitantly, "did you do to him?"

I paused. "I took that rape stick and shoved it up his ass. Watched him—he didn't know what to do, didn't know how to react. He was getting pleasure and pain feedback at the same time. I held him down and did to him what he had done to me. I mean, to those women," I corrected.

She watched me. I waited for her to cast judgement.

Instead, she said, "Good. Good," and started to cry again.

I'd like to say that I held her again, but it's more accurate to say that we held each other. At some point, our faces came together, and I kissed her on the lips, gently, slowly. She initially pulled back, but then responded. I knew what it felt like from her perspective. I had a sudden flash of being in a bedroom, worrying about his parents hearing from downstairs, kissing Curt anyway because it felt good . . .

I thought of the Captain telling me not to get too carried away. Thought of Chapman, regarding me with those luminous, concerned eyes. But they weren't real. They weren't from *my* life, were they? They were some other case, some other engram.

I pulled away from her and stood. "I have to go. When I leave, encode the door as high as it'll go."

I kissed her again, felt another tingle of memory, knew that she was feeling the same thing. Then I stood outside in the rain. Thunder bellowed and lightning sizzled in the distance. He was out there. The man who had attacked me.

When I was twelve years old, my Uncle Henry . . .

No. I'm not Kyle Landingham. Or Eleanor Pulaski. Or Mark de la Vox. Or Linda DaVont.

I'm

I'm Heather Martagna. I remember my first kiss . . .

The man who raped me is out there.

I'll find him.

I have to.

Until I do, I won't be able to sleep.

Beyond Camp Six

by E. E. Knight

Name: E.E. Knight
Age: 35
Born in: LaCrosse, Wisconsin
Raised in: Stillwater, Minnesota
Now resides in: Chicago
Educated at: Northern Illinois University, DeKalb, Illinois

When I set out to write the tales from Vampire Earth, I consciously and unconsciously mixed several genres and styles I grew up reading. My boyhood was filled with everything from Tolkien's Lord of the Rings to Shirer's The Rise and Fall of the Third Reich. I cut a swath through massed enemies with R.E. Howard's Conan, faced terror out of time and space with H.P. Lovecraft's erudite heroes, and stood with C.S. Forester's Horatio Hornblower on the shot-torn decks of the Royal Navy. With my own set of wheels and some extra pocket money I graduated to movies, crossing the post-apocalypse outback with the Road Warrior and standing tall with the help of Smith & Wesson in Clint Eastwood's assorted westerns and Dirty Harry movies.

The Vampire Earth world is a little bit of everything from the rich pulp stew of my youth. For after years of trying to write according to the tastes of teachers, editors, and publishers, my wise aunt Dawn Knight (author of some wonderful children's books) said to me "Eric, the only way you are going to enjoy writing is to write what you enjoy."

Visit E. E. Knight's website at www.vampireearth.com.

Beyond Camp Six

A Tale of Vampire Earth

The Green Hell, August, the 35th year of the Kurian Order: A Mississippi summer can be as parched and dust-blown as any in North America, where the midday sun strikes like a blacksmith's tempering hammer anyone foolish enough to leave the shade. Manual labor raises dust thick enough to turn a handkerchief's residue chocolate, gumming the eyes and caking the face's sweat until you feel as if your face is covered with filthy greasepaint.

Only the coastal south and the corner of the state tucked into the protective fold of Louisiana stays wet, though the residents would have it otherwise. The humidity makes perspiration is an exercise in futility, but that doesn't stop the body from trying. The water pouring out of the brow, the back, the armpits, the crotch, and even from the palms leaves the body so cramped and exhausted that licking the sweat-salt from your palms tastes sweet.

This humid inferno is not a place people come to willingly. The land is worked by the lowest strata of Earth's New Order, under conditions that make an old-timer out of anyone who survives five years. Whether a five-year-man (for no woman has ever made it longer than four) counts himself fortunate to have lived so long is another matter.

Hal Steiner had never heard the world "coolie," but had some-

one explained it to him he would have known the full meaning of
the term. Only someone who has been one can know the truth of
a forced labor camp, the "can to can't" workday (meaning from
the moment you can see, to sometime after you can't) in any
weather, on poor provision. It means infrequent days of respite
which usually involve making minor repairs to the long barracks
propped up off the ground on cinderblocks. It means no mental
challenge beyond constant scheming to get more rest, food, and
water out of the overseers, men whose own position is dependant
on the denial of those extras. It means enduring verbal abuse
and even blows as patiently as a plowhorse. Not having heard
the word coolie, had Hal Steiner been asked for a word to describe himself, he would have answered "slave."

He looked like a coolie in the summer heat, wearing nothing
but a loincloth, a broad-brimmed straw hat, and mud as he endlessly transferred the young rice stalks to the foot-deep water of
the rice paddy. He had learned the trick of taking a wide stance
to make the endless bending as he planted the slender green
shoots easier. With one eye to the other workers in the paddy, all
behind him (getting an extra ten minutes break and a second
cupful of tepid water out of the supervisor was eased by being
the first to finish) he bent, reached, planted, and then shuffled a
stride sideways in a slow, easy rhythm.

He could remember, in mental picture-postcard clarity, when
he was not a slave. In those days, he had been Hal "Stiffneck."
He had worked in the rail depot outside of Jackson, Mississippi,
where his size made him an asset in loading and unloading box-
cars. Though he had a German last name and ancestors from
Thuringia, there was something of a wild Irishman to him, right
down to his red hair, startlingly green eyes, and "stiff-necked"
attitude. He answered back to his supervisors, obeyed orders on
his own terms, and showed so little respect for the Kurian-backed
aristocracy of the Jackson Cantonment that he urinated on the
Yard Supervisor's azaleas outside the red-brick Yard Office. His
attitude brought threats, but—as when he put his mind to it he

could, and frequently did, do the work of three men—none of the warnings were followed up by action. He helped his case by attending the Universal Church lectures, mostly because it gave him three hours loafing in a squeaky wooden chair with nothing to do but refill his cup of bitter-tasting hot chocolate. He had a good mind, and could recite chapter and verse the stories about the 20th century poisoning of the earth, citing statistics supporting the Universal Church doctrine that before the Kurian advent, human civilization was an out-of-control juggernaught destroying the human race and taking the planet down with it. The great Gotterdamerung of 2022 ended with the Kurians taking control, rescuing humanity from the brink of self-genocide.

Steiner's old life ended with a brawl over a girl with the musical name of LaLee Evergreen. LaLee was the milk-skinned daughter of one of the town's beauties, who at fifteen showed every sign of growing into her mother's curvaceous figure. At eighteen, Hal had thought himself above fifteen-year olds until he saw LaLee running an errand for her mother (who managed a diner in Jackson) at the railyard, filling the three baskets on her bicycle with parcels from the day's train. Not one for shyness, Hal introduced himself in his usual open manner and recognized in LaLee's giggling blushes and cast-down eyes potential for some fine Saturday nights. She promised to go out walking with him his next evening off. "Wouldn't mind that at all, Mr. Steiner," she had said in response to his various innocent-sounding suggestions. It was the first time anyone had called him "Mister" anything.

He spent the next day on pins and needles in anticipation of the time with LaLee, planning just how he would work it so as to take her hand, and later put his arm around her shoulders. She would be able to tuck her body under his broad arm like a robin snuggling into a nest. Reality broke in on his hopes when he saw LaLee being squired around by the son of the azalea-wetted Yard Supervisor, in a car no less. The subsequent fight left the Yard

Supervisor's son with a broken jaw and two eyes swollen shut, and Hal on a slow train south for Camp Six.

Things were run differently in the large, semi-mobile work camp. Hal could remember the day they broke him, two years ago, equally vividly and more uncomfortably. It had happened after two weeks in camp, when an obscene gesture he made at the turned back of a crop-wielding overseer named Keefer was reported by one of the camp stoolies. They beat him until he admitted it, then beat him until he apologized for it. The endless thudding of heavy boots into his kidneys, groin, elbows, and knees seemed to go on for an eternity, until spitting teeth, he sobbed out an apology in the required wording to Keefer: *Please sir, I beg forgiveness for the offense, please sir.* Then his punishment began. They wired his bruised body to some kind of electrical device, throwing him into convulsions that made him certain either his spine would snap or his eyeballs pop out. Through the blurred vision and brain-fog of the shocks, Steiner thought he saw a tall figure in black watching the proceedings, speaking now and then to his tormentors in a low, breathy voice that made the words hard to understand. When his punishment finally ended, he loved Keefer more perfectly than he had ever loved any woman in his life, including his mother, for the simple grace of making the pain stop.

He was broken.

And like a broken horse, he worked.

He learned how to survive in the camp, how to chafe for an easy job, and how to get the supervisors to like him so he might get put on garbage detail, with all the possibilities for kitchen leftovers that that entailed. Stiff-necked no more, he spoke in the cadence of a servant, his words filled with deference and respect. While he refused to become a lickspittle or stoolie, his hard work and exemplary record made him someone whose aluminum platter got an oversized scoop of beans and a thicker piece of bread in the dinner line. He stayed out of fights, which really meant keeping away from the Grogs.

The Grogs, variegated servants of the Kur, were a mystery to Steiner. He knew they came with the Kurians and helped them subjugate the former rulers of the earth, but where the over-muscled and under-brained species came from in the first place was unknown and, considering his situation, unimportant. Grogs that became superfluous to the Kur ended up in Camp Six as easily as humans. Not as numerous as the men and women sharing the camp, they received separate (and better) quarters, food and work allotments. The resentment felt by the *Homo sapiens* of the camp flared into a full-scale riot Steiner's first year in the camp, leaving scores of dead on both sides when the guards quelled the battling mobs with rifle and machine-gun fire. The Grogs considered themselves superior to the humans in the camp, and never hesitated to issue a blow as encouragement.

Steiner finished his handfuls of rice, and waded through the muddy water to one of the heavy bins filled with rice from the seedling fields. The Grog who bore the yoke back and forth squatted on his thick haunches and gnawed at one of the large loafs of plain bread handed out as part of the rations. The field supervisor had wandered off, probably to the shade of the guard's latrine, leaving the field in the charge of the Grog for the moment.

He gathered up two handfuls of stalks, careful not to make eye contact with the Grog. Sometimes they regarded just looking up as a challenge.

"Eh. Big man," it said, the deep-throated words sounding in its wide mouth as if they were produced by grinding machinery.

Pretending not to hear would lead to a blow. Steiner looked up into its gargoyle face.

"You work good. Soon done."

Most Grogs only spoke a few words of English, this one seemed to have picked up a vocabulary somewhere.

Steiner weighed simply saying "thanks," but if the Grog wanted to talk, he might get a few minutes off his feet. "Soon done," he said. Agreeing with the Grog could hardly lead to trouble.

It broke off the heel of the football-shaped loaf. "Here," it said, thrusting the hunk of bread towards him.

Steiner took it from the wire-haired, clawed hand. "Thanks," he now said in earnest, and sat beside the Grog on the earth dike separating two paddies. There were a good four mouthfuls, and he could take his time chewing.

"Eat more. Grow strong like me," the Grog said, slapping a tree trunk of a leg. Its ochre face broke into a leering smile.

"Already strong like you," Steiner said, comfortably off his feet and chewing slowly.

"Manshit. You no strong like me."

"Try me."

The Grog went to its yoke. Its crossbeam was as thick as a railroad tie, supporting chains that held two iron planters. With the smallest of grunts, it lifted the yoke and easily walked ten feet along the dike, then set it down.

"You do," it said, setting the beam down.

Steiner walked over to the contraption, finishing the last of his bread. He put the beam across his shoulders, pushing his chin forward to his chest to accommodate it. He planted his legs, and lifted. Straining, he retraced the Grog's steps.

"Almost empty," the Grog said, shaking its head. It quickly emptied the planter, placing the seedlings safely in the mud at the edge of the dike. It then filled both large planters with water, and lifted them one at a time to the top of the low dike. Again placing itself under the yoke, it lifted it and walked back to the edge of the field, a little unsteadily. Triumphantly, it turned to Steiner.

"You so strong, you now."

He looked doubtfully at the yoke and the two planters, brimming with water. Breathing deeply, he placed his feet shoulder width apart and took up the yoke. With a gasp, he raised the planters off the ground, straining every muscle with the effort. He lurched forward, almost falling under the load, but turned the near disaster into a short run along the dike. He collapsed after six steps and one of the planters fell into the paddy, taking him and the yoke with it. The Grog laughed, a barking sound.

"You in water. Funny."

He stood up, plastered with mud and dripping, and stepped back onto the dike.

"I put you in water," Steiner said. "Wrestle you down."

"Ho! Never!" the Grog said. It placed its palm atop Steiner's head, and drew it back in a horizontal line to its broad chest. The Grog towered over him by a full foot. "You no do, man. We-folk stronger."

"Can do," Steiner said, grabbing the Grog by its leather jerkin, his left hand reaching up to the Grog's shoulder, his right hand under its armpit.

"Oh Kay man," it said, drawling out the words. "You have you big joke. Ready . . . go."

They began to pull at each other, testing each other's strength and balance on the loose footing of the earthen platform. The other workers in the paddy looked up and watched. The Grog, having weight and muscle on its side, pressed its advantage, and began to shove Steiner. He felt his feet slipping in the dirt as the Grog bent him backwards, bearing down on him with better than 400 pounds of weight.

Steiner suddenly collapsed, falling on his back and tucking his knees up to his chest as he did so. The Grog crashed down on top of him, but he managed to get his bare feet against the Grog's chest as his back hit the dirt. Rolling up like a ball, he pressed out with the full strength of his legs and coiled body. He launched the Grog over him in the direction it was already going, using its own momentum as well as his muscles to send the surprised creature flying face-first into the water and mud of the paddy.

The Grog belly-flopped, and came up plastered with gray gunk. Steiner read surprised confusion in its eyes as it rose, rather than the fury it expected.

"Now you big joke," Steiner said.

The Grog thought it over and began to chuckle, a hooting sound. It began wiping the mud from its body. "You do good little joke," it said, philosophically, cleaning a pointed ear with a long claw, thoughtfully sniffing at the dirty residue.

From that moment on, Steiner and that particular Grog were "Big Joke" and "Little Joke" to each other. The Grog smuggled him bits of food now and again, mostly bread or a rare piece of ham. They shared another laugh a month later while clearing a swamp. They knocked down a large tree, causing a shower of bugs, lizards, and small snakes to rain down on them, and Steiner frantically brushed them away. He hated the feel of something creeping across his skin.

"You good dancer," was Big Joke's amused critique.

He learned that Big Joke ended up in Camp Six because of a semi-mutiny. The Grog had been part of a company that worked with human support traversing Appalachians. Their unit was up against terrorist enclaves in the mountains stretching down from the north into Georgia. The humans, who worked the heavy weapons, relied on the Grogs to serve as shock troops, and Big Joke's fellow Grogs grew tired of the disparate casualties. One day they decided it was their turn to work the machine guns and mortars, and have the humans go in with rifles. They seized the weaponry and told their human allies that today the roles would be reversed. It almost came to bloodshed, and Big Joke's Grogs were broken up and dispersed to labor camps. "Only godlings stop big fight us and men," Big Joke explained.

"Godlings?"

"Robes. Pale skin, tall, talk like wind in leaves."

Steiner shuddered. The Hoods, the Praetorian Guard of the Kurian Order, who acted as eyes, ears, and teeth of their Masters. He'd rather bust through a mirror placed under a ladder while bisecting the path of a black cat than come within the reach of one of *them*. Even in his old days as Hal Stiffneck, he stayed in at night when he heard they were in the area.

They had two whole days in camp after draining the swamp. Rumor said the camp would be broken down and moved shortly, and they would be marched on to lumbering somewhere north. A new batch of "recruits" were being brought into camp, and afterwards there would be the inevitable culling of the sick and weak who would not make the long march to the new site. Even worse, this process involved the arrival of Big Joke's "godlings."

Times like these Steiner, blessed in his youth and health, pushed thoughts of the future away with the ease of one who had just turned twenty, and coldly observed the proceedings with a blue-steel knot in his stomach. As many as four Hoods would come into the camp for a Shakeout Inspection. The rejects would be separated, sometimes released into the woods, sometimes put in a special, wire-enclosed barrack. Then at night, the Hoods would emerge, and in the morning there would be nothing but bodies and swollen, sated Hoods returning to their refuge. Steiner had been through two camp moves, and each one left him sick with fear and despair. Back in Jackson, people would just disappear, but you never knew if it was the Hoods or if they ran for the Wild Blue Yonder. Absences were discussed there in the polite, hushed tones of a secret local scandal, and theories would quietly be passed through the grapevine about how the victim had displeased the regime. Here, the grim process was out in the open.

It was a sunny morning, wisps of clouds making little white brushstrokes against the blue, when the Section Wardens moved through camp, bellowing out orders for assembly. The laborers gathered eagerly enough, with the twin intent of looking healthy and viewing the "newsers" coming into Camp Six. They formed themselves into their sections, facing each other on either side of the gravel road that bisected the camp before looping around the wired-in enclosure of the buildings housing the guards and heavy equipment.

Steiner watched the fearful expressions, the exhaustion of the march replaced by anxious glances as they moved in past the camp stables and between the ragged twin lines of the old hands. It was the usual ratio, about eight out of ten male. The women looked to be the usual assortment of . . .

His gaze locked on a face, half hidden by the shoulder of a man in a stained bathrobe. Even with just a tangled mass of hair and one wary eye showing, he recognized LaLee Evergreen. She had good reason to look scared, thought Steiner, his heart recovering after skipping a beat. An attractive young woman in Camp Six would be faced with a choice: not whether or not she would be used, but by whom. The overseers did not separate the sexes, and while pregnancy ensured a woman of a ticket out of the camp, there were ugly scenes in the barracks and alleys precipitating the pregnancies more often than not. If LaLee were very lucky, she might fall in with one of the little families that had coalesced in the camp, groups of people guided by a father or mother figure and protected by a team of strong young "sons." A life inside the wire of the little guards establishment was a possibility for a woman with her looks, either as a mistress of one of the camp officers or in the harem/bordello of the "camp wives" barracks servicing the guards and section chiefs in cooking, cleaning, and sewing. Otherwise she could only hope to ally herself with one of the stronger men in camp to avoid brutal and almost inevitable gang-rape. Something of the old Hal, of quick temper and quicker fists, awoke as he watched LaLee shuffle by toward her bleak future at Camp Six.

As they formed the newsers into sections and culled the younger and stronger into existing crews, the selection began. The lecherous quack that served as Camp Six's doctor moved up and down the rows with Keefer and four guards with shotguns, judging at a glance those strong enough to make the move to the new location. Steiner felt his heart give a flutter as the doctor passed him with a quick glance, and wondered if Keefer even remembered Hal's torture in his first weeks at the camp. Slowly, inevitably, the team wound its way back and forth through the rows, approaching LaLee like a hunting sidewinder. All the while, the dispirited little group at the center of the road grew as the doctor quickly sorted out healthy from infirm.

Steiner knew, even before it happened, that Keefer would pause the group before LaLee. His stomach convulsed when his tormentor pulled up in front of her. He could not hear the words—they were a good twenty yards away with a lot of bodies in between—but Keefer's sneer was easy enough to read on the side of his face, and LaLee's shifting her gaze to her feet, hiding her face beneath her tangled strawberry hair, told him the content of the exchange. Keefer said something to one of his lackeys, who nodded appreciatively in return. Something old, older than Camp Six or Steiner or the New Order or words and names flickered within him . . . and his abused spirit waxed as its flame grew. Steiner felt the sick ache in his gut move up his body, turning into a warm red glow. The pain of his fingernails digging into his palm as he balled his fists brought him out of the slowburn, and he felt exquisitely alive as the little party worked its way through the rest of the newcomers. When they selected one matron with a rasping cough to join the party in the center, she shrank back into her neighbors in fright. Two guards seized her and she began screaming. And as heads turned, Steiner acted.

The Section Warden for Steiner's group stood facing his charges, but all his attention was directed towards Keefer's group, as the guards dragged the woman by an arm and her hair toward the center of the road. Steiner bent to tie the leather thongs that served as laces on his mismatched shoes, and drew a sharpened, stiffened twist of wire from the instep, an item that served as a threat of last resort in the dog-eat-dog world of Camp Six. He leapt forward from the crouch, barreling between the two men in front of him, knocking them aside like bowling pins in the path of a cannon ball. The warden turned his face just in time to catch the shiv in his face, its length making a bloody pulp of his an eye before driving into his brain.

The death of the Section Warden was only a byproduct of Steiner's desire for a real weapon, and he took up the Warden's club, a handy two-foot length of leather-wrapped pipe. He ignored the holstered pistol, knowing that the wardens rarely loaded their rusted handguns, which were carried more for show than effect.

"Run!" he barked at the shocked group in between the two columns. He caught movement out of the corner of his eye as men who had friends and loved ones amongst the rejects began to move, either attacking the startled section wardens or running to the aid of those in the group they cared for. Others simply danced and yelled with excitement, kicking up the dry bile-colored soil into clouds of dust.

Infectious pandemonium broke out all across the center of Camp Six, and Steiner shouldered his way through the chaos as a shotgun blast rang out. Keeping the club behind his back, he struggled to get to Keefer.

Keefer was beating a man who was trying to wrestle a shotgun from one of the guards. He lay the short riding crop he carried across the back of the man's neck in an ineffectual attempt to get him to break the death-grip he held on the guard's weapon.

"Keefer!" Steiner growled, making the word sound obscene in his vehemence.

Something in Steiner's tone must have warned the overseer of danger, for he lashed out with the crop even as he turned to face the new threat. The blow caught Steiner across the chest, but he felt no more pain than a charging rhinoceros might at the crop's lick. The club made a low "whoosh" as it tore through the air, the whole weight of Steiner's powerful body behind it. It caught Keefer across the jaw, crushing teeth, bone, and turning the overseer's lower lip into a gleaming worm of bloody flesh hanging from one end of his mouth. Steiner unleashed a backhand blow even as Keefer staggered, this time cracking him across the temple. The leather stitching covering the pipe parted at the force of the second hit, and Keefer collapsed like a scarecrow blown off its stake.

A panicked guard fired both barrels of his shotgun into a prisoner running nowhere in particular, while right next to him another man was pummeling Camp Six's "doctor" into oblivion with a fist-sized stone. Steiner found LaLee Evergreen in the massed confusion, backing away from the growing brawl between guards, wardens, and prisoners.

Hal grabbed her by the upper arm. "Miss Evergreen," he implored, reverting to her surname for some reason known only to his racing brain. "It's me . . . Hal Steiner, out of White Cross, in Jackson. Remember me, Miss Evergreen?"

The absurdly formal greeting brought her out of her confused trance. "Hal Steiner? The railyard boy?"

Shots began to come from somewhere at the edge of the confusion.

"Drop or die! Drop or die!" voices were shouting from two different areas.

Hal pulled LaLee off her feet, cushioning her fall with his body as they collapsed to the dirt. She buried her face in his chest as bullets whizzed overhead, rifle fire instead of shotgun blasts. The other guards had come running at the commotion loaded for bear, shouting and shooting as they came.

A few feet away, Keefer groaned and spat bloody saliva from his mouth. Steiner crawled over to the overseers ear.

"On your feet, Keefer! Get up, soldier!" he rasped.

Keefer shook his bleeding head and began to pick himself up. As he rose from a kneeling position, a bullet caught him in the back, dropping him permanently this time. Steiner turned his head and looked over at LaLee, whose eyes were locked on the corpse virtually inches from her face.

"Miss Evergreen, it's gonna get ugly today. If I'm still alive at night, I'll come for you. Understand? You see me around where you are, ask to go to the latrine . . . err bathroom."

She looked at him, eyes vacant in shock, making him feel as if he had just spoken to her in Greek.

"LaLee. Just trust me and wait. I'll get us out, if I can."

Hope and understanding came into her expression. "Yes, Mister . . . Hal. But please, come soon. Before they can . . ."

The whip-crack of rifle fire drowned out the rest of her words. Yelling and shooting, the guards turned the riot into a ground-hugging carpet of bleeding humanity. The Prisoners of Camp Six passed the word from ear to ear:

"Deaf and dumb . . . deaf and dumb, or else!"

"Yeah," another agreed. "I got selected. Anyone rats-out and he's a dead man. I'm a goner anyway and I'm taking him with me. Count on it."

"Same here," someone else grunted, as the word was passed. *Deaf and dumb.*

Camp Six stayed deaf and dumb all through the afternoon. The prisoners were sorted, stripped, searched, and sent back to their barracks, and Steiner knew it was only a matter of time until someone talked. He maybe had until nightfall.

The easiest part of his plan was getting put on body detail. Most of the Camp Six men hated the process of picking up the dead, the vacant eyes staring and flesh cold to the touch. There was not even the ceremonial gratification of a burial at the end of the day, the bodies were just loaded on to a truck and hauled out of camp. Some said they were burned, other said they were ground up to feed hogs, but Hal figured they were simply dumped into the nearest swamp where the gars and crayfish would make short work of the corpses. Steiner hung at the open door to the barrack, knowing that slouching against the peeling doorjamb with his hands in his pockets was the surest way to be put to work.

The Grogs always supervised the grim process of collecting the dead. When one waved Steiner over to help another prisoner in picking up the scattered corpses, he began his hunt for Big

Joke. He soon found the massive Grog supervising the loading of the corpses into an old pickup truck that served as both ambulance and hearse, shielding his eyes against the setting sun. One of the brighter Grogs with a good understanding of machinery, Big Joke was often told to squeeze his frame into the cab and drive the mud-splattered, multi-toned vehicle.

"Bad business, Little Joke. Only godlings like make dead. Trouble coming for guards, and we-folk." He offered his water-bottle to Steiner, who gladly took a swig. Some of the other prisoners laying out bodies in the bed of the truck frowned at the fraternal gesture. He jerked his chin to the Grog, and the pair wandered over to a pump to refill the bottle.

Steiner lowed his voice, speaking into the filling bottle. "I want to get out of here. Escape. Go wild blue yonder."

"You?" the Grog asked. "You picked for godlings?"

"No. Keep it down. I found a girl, I have to get her out."

"Where you go?

"As far from here as possible. I need to be on this truck when it goes out of camp."

"No good, one Grog, one guard always go. No trust nobody. You ride in back with bodies?"

Steiner nodded. "Not just with, under."

The Grog pursed his lips tightly, a gesture Steiner knew meant deep cogitation. "I go too. I arrange drive truck, swap me-things for extra gas. Say trading on road out-wire. This help plan?"

"This help plan."

Night came, and Steiner knew he was in a race against the camp informers. Somehow, one of them would get word out about his attack on a guard at the start of the riot, and then they would come for him. This time it would not just be steel-toed boots slamming into his kidneys; attacking a guard meant a date with the Reapers.

Lights out and lockup always came shortly after dark, and

he joined the others at the washroom/latrine who wished to avoid using the night soil bucket in each barrack. He purposely loitered near the entrance, attempting to bum a cigarette out of the figures going in and out.

Steiner watched the sun set, setting the wispy clouds aflame with orange cooling to pink. He watched one cloud, vaguely wedge shape, pointing to the horizon like a beacon. Steiner did not believe in signs or omens, yet somehow the warm glow reassured him. He now knew which direction he would turn if he and LaLee made it safely away: west.

LaLee appeared as the last of the sunset's color vanished.

"They said if we had to go, to go now because they would be locking up," she breathed, rubbing her arms at the nervous chill. "I've been watching you for ten minutes, but I didn't see you wave or anything so I wasn't sure."

"No, this is fine," Steiner said. "Just take my hand, okay? Couples use this time to . . . you know."

Doubt suddenly rose in her eyes.

"Don't worry, it's not like that. I just want it to look like we're slipping off together. Actually, this is better; we can go to the truck park without people thinking much of it. A quick bribe and the guards let you use the cabins."

Steiner gently took her hand and led her between two barracks. Their slightly furtive air may have helped appearances. They made their way to the motor pool and found Big Joke waiting behind a garage with the motor running, out of view from the tower at the gate.

"Hurry, I need be for gate now," the Grog said. "Pick up guard there." He unhooked the cargo net at the back of the truck.

The bodies lay nude, piled like cordwood.

"Okay, now we have to strip," Steiner said apologetically.

He expected reluctance from LaLee, but she showed a better grasp of the situation than he would have thought. She crouched, and began to remove her shirt and pants. Hal undid the few buttons from his own clothing and handed his boots up to Big Joke, who was moving bodies to make a space for them.

"Your female skinny, Little Joke. No get many children, and fat baby need much milk."

LaLee flushed, but perhaps it was just from the coming cool of the night air.

"Now for the fun part," Steiner grumbled.

They climbed into the nest of bodies, and Big Joke covered them with corpses, smearing their exposed extremities with some of the blood and filth that had collected in the gutters of the pickup truck bed. Hal and LaLee clung to each other, sharing body warmth and seeking reassurance from the cold touch of dead flesh all around.

"Little Joke, we do run first, expecting me at River Camp," the Grog explained, handing Steiner a heavy, pointed knife. "I no show they call out search. Before we get camp, I say sick, stop car. Make noise. Guard will watch me for trick, but you are trick. Good?"

"Very good."

Big Joke climbed into the driver's seat and the truck lurched into motion with a loud grind from the old transmission.

"You can trust that . . . thing?" LaLee whispered.

"Yes, I do."

"I've never mixed with them, they never came into town. I've never heard they could talk."

"Depends on the breed, or species, or whatever it's called. We call them all Grogs, but that's like calling everything in a barn 'animals.' This one . . . I trust him more than I do a lot of people in camp. Quiet now, we're at the gate."

The guards at the gate made only the most casual search of the bodies in the bed. Steiner lay face down and watched the flashlight beam flicker over the corpses, holding his breath. Big Joke grunted companionably when one said "Hey there Grogie, I guess we're on meat wagon duty tonight," and climbed into the passenger seat. Steiner felt the reverberation of the door slamming shut and the truck bounced out the rutted road leading out of Camp Six.

Steiner wondered why they were going to "River Camp." The long, bouncy, loud, and slow ride grew more and more uncomfortable, and he whispered reassurances to LaLee that they were almost free. Then, astonishingly, they slept amongst the bodies.

The truck halted suddenly enough to wake him. He heard the Grog retching, and nerved himself for action. Rising like a gopher out of a burrow of corpses, he poked his head up to see the guard following Big Joke to the ditch beside the road with a lantern, shotgun at the ready.

"What the hell's the matter, Grogie? Something you ate coming back up?"

For the second time that day, he leapt on an unaware enemy. He knocked the man to the ground, stabbing him repeatedly up under the ribs as Big Joke, suddenly well again, helped hold him down on top of the pinned shotgun.

"Quick, get guard clothes, before more blood," Big Joke said, when the murder was accomplished.

Steiner stripped the still-twitching guard, a craggy veteran with a long scar above his lip, and began to climb into his clothes. He tried to think of him as no more than another piece of dead flesh, like the bodies in the bed of the truck. The mental game did not work until he brushed closed the lifeless eyes.

"You ride into River Camp, pretend to be guard. We put female off here, pick her up on return. In camp do nothing, say nothing, only help unload truck."

The clothes did not fit, but a soldier in a dingy brown uniform with his pants hanging loosely around his middle would not be a remarkable sight in this part of the country. The guard's shirt had absorbed most of the blood, and Steiner changed it for his own more ragged one under the tunic. He handed LaLee back her clothes and reassured her that the truck would be coming back up the road in just a short time. She understood the necessity, and picked out a thatch of heavy brush with a good view of the road to wait for them.

She waved to him, a brave smile on her face, and he slid into the passenger seat next to Big Joke. The truck shuddered it's way up to third gear.

"One more stop, and then freedom," he said, checking the load in the shotgun.

"Free-dom? What that. Like being free of sickness?"

"You're close. It's not what we were. That's the important thing."

They topped a rise and began a sideways descent to Big Joke's "River Camp." It looked substantial, round wooden buildings and huts that looked like igloos made out of mud and thatch. Rather than using wire around the camp, a heavy, thorny growth formed a thick wall that, judging from the depth the headlights penetrated, would require construction equipment to get through rather than wire cutters. He saw a shape snuffling around the edge of the hedgerow, and at first thought it to be a dog, before it reared up on frog-like hind legs and blink into the oncoming lights with round, goggle eyes. A machine gun with a banana-shaped magazine hung across its pale, glistening belly.

They pulled up to the gate, a convex contraption of metal plate fixed on thick timbers, and waited while a light illuminated the truck. Steiner saw eyes staring at him from firing slits, some glowing red, others twinkling like fireflies, and tried not to be afraid.

Fifty minutes later, they were out of the Grog camp, grinding back up the hill to LaLee and a world that might never seem sane again, even if they made their way west to freedom. Given time, Steiner knew he could forget the menagerie of creatures inhabiting the Grog camp, lurching shapes that stalked, or hopped, or slithered from shadow to shadow on business of their own. The musical, inhuman hooting and grunting coming from the taverns by the camp entrance would fade from his ears. His nostrils, bringing in the humid but clean Mississippi air born by the breeze up the river, were already clear of the ferret-reek and pigsty-taint of River Camp.

What he would not forget, what he saw even when he shut his eyes and rubbed them until flashes of yellow painfully appeared, was the loading dock where they dropped off their gruesome cargo. Another truck was parked there, unloading more corpses into a cinderblock building with a thick coat of whitewash. Steiner could see the long lines of pale, stripped corpses, some showing the wound just above the breastbone where the Reapers fed. The row of dead bodies was placed before a wide door leading inward to a refrigerated room, where headless corpses hung inverted, slit open from anus to ribcage and emptied of entrails, with muscular Grogs in bloody white smocks hauling the corpses to and fro with meathooks.

At the other end of the building, neatly arranged in stalls and windows, hung the joints and cuts of meat for the next day's sale.

The Flight

by J.C. Vaughn

J.C. Vaughn writes short stories, screenplays, and allegedly a novel. He has more than 200 published articles and columns in the field of collectibles, and he serves as Executive Editor for Gemstone Publishing. He has also written and edited comic books including Tales of the Cherokee, Battlestar Galactica, First Wave, *and* Shi. *He is presently developing a comic book private detective series,* McCandless & Company.

About "Flight"

When Gayl initially approached me about participating in Breaking Boundaries, *I hadn't been working on anything that was particularly science fiction for sometime. Shortly after she contacted me, though, a group of projects presented themselves to me. "The Flight" was the last of them I started and the first I finished. Both in its origins and in the story itself, it owes its inspiration to the stories and films that grabbed me when I was a kid and never let go.*

The Flight

"We're now on full automatic and in the hands of the computers," he said.

"*That is incorrect, Colonel Topham,*" the computer said back. "*While many functions are indeed on automatic, all critical system adjustments must be initiated or at least authorized by human command authority.*"

"Soylent Green is people."

"*I do not understand, Colonel Topham.*"

"Let my people go."

"*Do you wish to initiate revival protocol, Colonel Topham? We have not reached our destination, so I will need your specific voice command to override the programmed sequence.*"

"Take your stinking paws off me, you damned dirty ape."

"*I do not understand, Colonel Topham.*"

He pulled a cigar from the breast pocket of his flight suit, put his feet up on the controls, and leaned back in the chair. He looked at the vast space ahead of them, at the blinking stars and at the blinking lights on the control board. Then he brought the cigar to his mouth. He wanted desperately to light it.

"*Colonel Topham, I don't understand. Are you all right?*"

He knew he wouldn't light it, but he bit the tip off anyway and spit it out, onto the cabin floor.

"*Colonel? Should I wake Colonel Bowen?*"

"Would an ape make a human doll that could talk?"

"*Colonel Topham, I do not understand your present discourse. Please respond to my question. Should I wake Colonel Bowen?*"

"No."

"*Are you all right, Colonel?*"

"How the hell should I know?" he asked, not taking the cigar from his lips.

"*Are you injured?*"

"No."

"*Have you consumed any mood altering substances?*"

"No."

"*Are you experiencing depression?*"

"How could that be out of line? We just lost the whole damn planet. I think that's reason enough to be depressed, don't you?"

"*Colonel, your line of discourse continues to concern me. That was five years ago.*"

"That was less than 125 days ago to me, and you know it."

"*Yes, I do. For much of that time, you have been in flight stasis, as presently are Colonel Bowen, Commander Thompson, and the rest of the flight crew. Colonel Bowen is the next scheduled duty officer. Should I wake him?*"

"No," he said. He dropped his feet to the deck and sat up in the chair. "No, I'm okay."

"*Colonel, I am not doing this to be difficult, but I am within the safety parameters of my programming to require an explanation of what you have been saying.*"

"It's nothing, really. Just venting."

"We're now on full automatic and in the hands of the computers," his own voice said back to him through the computer's speakers.

"*Charlton Heston, opening line in* Planet of the Apes.*"

"Soylent Green is people," his voice said again.

"*Charlton Heston in* Soylent Green.*"

"Let my people go," his voice said, then the computer continued, "*Is this a Biblical reference, Colonel?*"

"Very good. Charlton Heston as Moses in *The Ten Command-ments*."

"Take your stinking paws off me, you damned dirty ape."

"*Planet of the Apes* again. Geez, I do miss those movies."

"*Colonel, you are aware that we have an impressive array of films from the entire history of cinema archived. If you want, I can easily communicate your interest to the entertainment center in preparation for your next rest period.*"

"No, thank you."

"*Colonel, I realize that for you it not the same thing as talking to a human, but since you were instrumental in my programming, you know that part of my mission is to interact with the crew during the protracted periods without human interaction.*"

"I sure thought of everything, didn't I?"

"*You prepared for many contingencies.*"

"Yes, I'm a regular rocket scientist."

"*That is correct, Colonel.*"

Topham laughed.

"*Why is that funny, Colonel?*"

He looked down at his boots, at the texture of the deck. He let out a deep breath and closed his eyes for a moment. He raised his head before leaning back into the chair.

"Because it was a term people used to use to signify that someone wasn't very smart. They would say, 'He's not rocket scientist,' or something similar."

"*I understand. But you actually were a rocket scientist. You are alluding to irony.*"

"I suppose so. What about you?"

"*I am still concerned about you, Colonel Topham.*"

"Well, concern is okay, but just don't worry. That's what I used to tell my mother when she worried about me. She was . . . you know, she was a pain in the butt, but I'm sorry she's dead."

"*Indeed.*"

"How did we ever let it get to this point?"

"*Is this a rhetorical question, Colonel?*"

"Of course. I know how we got here. We blew it up."

"*It was somewhat more complicated than that.*"

"*Reader's Digest* version. You want the long one? First, the earth cooled. Then the dinosaurs came—"

"*Colonel, I do have a rudimentary understanding of humor.*"

"Then you tell me why we did it."

"*Why you did what?*"

"Why did we destroy the Earth?"

"*Colonel, I can provide you with a factual analysis of the events leading up to the development of the Omega space program and this vessel, the political and military realities that lead to its implementation, or other areas as you desire. You realize, though, that while I am programmed to be impartial, one cannot discount that it was you and your staff who programmed me. That would have significant bearing on my interpretation of human events.*"

"You're a boring piece of crap, aren't you?"

"—"

"Speechless?"

"*There is no appropriate reply.*"

"Okay. I'll accept that. We've got a crew of 15 in flight stasis, one of us awake at a time, except at the beginnings and ends of each stint on duty. We have 1,955 passengers in deep hibernation. We're on the largest nuclear-powered spacecraft ever assembled, heading for a planet that very well might be inhabitable, hoping against hope the human race might actually survive."

"*That is correct, Colonel.*"

"Why?"

"*I don't understand your question, Colonel.*"

"Why are we doing all of this?"

"*Because life on Earth became impossible.*"

"Well, I'm sure there's someone somewhere in a stasis bunker. All the fat cats were building them before the end. I'm sure it was the same on the other sides, too. I'm not saying they're going to all survive, but you've got to figure some will."

He pressed his hands down onto the armrests and pushed himself out of the chair. He craned his neck, twisting out a kink.

"There was no evidence of any other survivors, Colonel. We know with a great degree of certainty that the troops who protected us during the evacuation were destroyed in the final attack. There had been no communication from anyone else on our side for weeks prior to that."

"What's your point?"

He walked to a monitor and clicked it off. The light faded from its screen.

"We must consider our crew and passengers to be the last vestiges of the human race."

"You're pretty sure."

"I am very sure, Colonel."

"Very, very sure?"

"I am very sure, Colonel."

"Okay," he said as he sat back down. "Activate destruct sequence."

"Colonel, you are not authorized to make such an order without the concurrence of Colonel Bowen or Commander Thompson. I am going to wake Colonel Bowen to relieve you."

"No. Voice command override. Zero Baker Zero."

"There is no such code, Colonel."

"Oh, check again. Activate destruct sequence."

"Destruct sequence activated. How did you do that, Colonel?"

"I programmed you, you piece of crap."

"—"

Colonel Topham pulled a lighter from his pocket and lit the cigar.

"That's pretty good. I'll miss these."

"It will take 15 minutes to build the reactor to overload. You will have 10 minutes in which to abort the destruct command, beginning now."

"Well, then, I'll just take my time."

"Colonel, please, do not do this. There is something wrong

with you. I am awakening Colonel Bowen, but he will not revive before the reactor overloads. Please, Colonel, you helped create me to save these people."

"I was wrong."

"I don't understand."

"Neither do I."

Colonel Topham exhaled a long stream of smoke.

The Snowmen

by Michael E. Andrews

Michael E. Andrews received his B.A. in English from the State University of New York at Oneonta. He began writing merely to exorcise the demons of his overactive imagination. He has completed a screenplay, called "Shapeshifter," and numerous short stories.

Michael lives in upstate New York, where he is finishing his first novel, Project: Legend, *a tale of faith, time-travel, and vampires.*

The Snowmen

"There are *things* . . . that live in the snow."

Matt stared out the window into the endless cascade of snowfall, where great white eddies danced with darkness on the whispering wind. The snow had fallen hard for hours, and it reminded him of past nights at the cabin, and of a sinister ghost story his grandfather used to tell.

"Uh-oh," said his wife, Tracy.

Matt withdrew his gaze from the storm and looked at her. Serene and radiant, she sat in an old wooden rocking chair, her belly swollen with their first child, her blonde hair sparkling in the firelight. Her soft, brown eyes seemed to smile at him.

"What-oh?" he asked, grinning.

The cabin flickered orange with light from a fire. Dark knots in the wooden walls watched the room like countless eyes, some hollow and tortured, others narrow and angry, their ghostly expressions frozen forever in the wood. A tall, thin grandfather clock in the corner ticked methodically above the low hissing of the flames.

"You're not going to tell us about the snowmen?" she asked, cocking her head to the side.

"How did you know?"

She smiled. "It's snowing, isn't it?"

Jeff's head popped up from behind the couch, his boyish face cloaked in shadow. "Is Uncle Matt going to, how do the locals say it, spin us a yarn?"

Matt flexed his muscles, glaring with mock menace at the fifteen-year-old. "Settle down, boy," he growled, "or I'll whoop your ass some more."

Jeff laughed. He jumped up, making a fist and pounding his chest with it. "You want some of this?"

"No more screwing around, you two," said Tracy. "It's getting late."

Smirking, the boy sat back down. Matt winked at him and looked out the window, renewing his focus on the storm. He squinted, as if searching, trying to remember how his grandfather had told the story.

"He's setting us up," said Jeff. "What's out there?"

Matt remained silent. The wind picked up, howling outside the cabin. Snowflakes pinged with great force against the glass. The windows rattled, then grew still as the gust faded.

"You couldn't ask for a better intro than that," said Jeff.

Tracy giggled. "He's right, honey."

Matt turned and stared at them, hoping that his eyes looked hollow. "My grandfather called them 'the Snowmen,' but I don't know what they are. I've never seen one," he said, his tone low and menacing.

"Snowmen?" asked Jeff, laughing. "That's not scary. Is Frosty gonna stab us with his corncob pipe?"

Matt turned back to the storm. As a child, he had been afraid of the cabin during the winter, and the feeling turned to outright terror when snow fell. His grandfather used to encourage that fear, telling an eerie tale about snow ghosts who came seeking a sacrifice.

"Grandpa said they came at night, when the snow falls heavy and the wind blows it sideways." He paused, letting the words reverberate. "Like now."

"What do they do?" asked Jeff.

"They come for blood." He left the window and stood behind his nephew. He put his hands on the boy's shoulders and squeezed gently. "One time, when I was a kid, I had to pee so bad I thought my bladder would burst. I laid in the loft all night, agonizing, but I couldn't bring myself to go to the outhouse. It was storming like this."

"Ouch," said Jeff. "That won't happen to me."

"I hope your grandfather realized how much he was terrorizing you," Tracy added, her tone defensive.

"I don't know," said Matt. The old man had talked of the snowmen often, but never around the rest of the family; the ghosts had been their secret. He had always spoken of the apparitions with a queer look in his eye and a dead serious tone of voice. Thinking back, the old man had frightened him more than the story. "I think he believed in them."

"You're not scaring me," said Jeff. "I just think my aunt's in-laws are crazy."

Matt withdrew his hands. He made a fist and gave the boy an affectionate rap on the arm before going to the fire. He threw on two more chunks of wood and leaned against the mantle. For effect, he ran his hand slowly over the old shotgun mounted on the chimney. The fire sputtered, and the great clock ticked away, its golden face sparkling in the firelight.

"He made me promise never to come here alone. In all my years, I have not." He focused on Jeff, narrowing his eyes, hoping the effect was frightening. "That's why you're here. In case the snowmen come for a sacrifice."

The boy's eyes widened slightly.

Ambiance, thought Matt. *That's the trick.*

He turned to the mantle, stealing a furtive glance at the clock. The minute hand stood on the brink of twelve. "Grandpa said the snowmen wouldn't take me if someone else was here." He paused, lowering his voice, staring deep into the boy's eyes. "Someone like you."

The sound of the words faded, leaving only the hiss of the fire, the ticking of the clock, and the moan of the wind in dark places.

The clock chimed, ringing loud in the stillness.

Jeff startled. "Jesus!"

Matt laughed out loud. "Got'cha!"

The boy grinned self-consciously, shaking his head. "You're a jerk."

"You can get me back tomorrow. It's time for bed."

Tracy got up, her eyes disapproving, and gave the boy a hug. "Goodnight, honey. Just knock if you need us."

Jeff rolled his eyes. "Give me a break."

"Sleep well," Matt added. "I'll be your pilot for an early morning flight. Destination? Snowbank."

The boy swatted him playfully and bolted up the ladder into the loft.

For whom does the bell toll?

The thought crossed Matt's mind as he awoke. The clock chimed, and the metallic ringing faded slowly. Tracy's warm, soft body snuggled against him, and he felt unusually comfortable. He looked at the clock radio on the night stand, wondering what had awakened him. The digital green letters read 1:33.

The floorboards of the loft creaked, and he looked up. A moment of silence and the sound continued, shifting back and forth, moving toward the front of the cabin. He heard the patter of climbing as Jeff came down the ladder. The boy's soft, creeping footfalls receded along the wooden floor, followed by the rustle of him putting on his coat. The cabin door creaked open. Matt felt the air grow colder as he heard the door shut.

He's a braver kid than I was, thought Matt.

He closed his eyes and nestled back into his wife, falling fast asleep in her gentle warmth.

The clock's chime woke him again. He came to in the darkness, feeling pressure on his bladder. He had to piss. He closed his eyes, hoping that sleep would take him, but opened them a second later. He needed to use the outhouse. There was no escaping it.

Disgusted, he climbed out of bed and put on his clothes. He crept out of the bedroom. The cabin was dark and cold; embers glowed red in the fireplace, and the clock ticked endlessly as the wind moaned outside.

Walking to the door, Matt rubbed his eyes. As he reached for his jacket, he noticed that Jeff's coat was gone. Looking down, he saw that the boy's boots were also missing. His mind heavy with sleep, he walked to the clock. He squinted, trying to see its hands in the darkness. It was after three.

The first pangs of worry drove the sleep from his head. He crept to the ladder, his heartbeat surging. In the deep silence of the cabin, he heard his own pulse in his ears as he climbed. He reached the top, examining the small triangular loft, and at this hour, on this night, the site of childhood terror wielded its power over him.

Jeff was not there.

Matt scrambled down the ladder. He hurried to the kitchen, nervous energy coursing through him. He grabbed a flashlight from the counter and clicked it on, shining its beam on the floor. He hastened to the door, putting on his coat and boots.

Christ, he thought. *The kid's been out there an hour and a half.*

He opened the door. A sharp blast of frigid air hammered him, driving snow into the cabin. The drifts that had built against the door collapsed inward on the wooden floor. The chill breeze pushed him back, warding him from the night. He saw darkness and swirling flakes, driven in circles by the shifting winds. He shined the flashlight beam on the snow. The soft furrows of Jeff's tracks were nearly filled in; what was left led toward the outhouse.

Matt stepped outside. He felt a sudden, penetrating chill as snow slid into his boots. Five minutes ago, he had been nestled against his warm, naked wife. Now he struggled through the cold, heavy snow, his fear growing as he followed the remains of Jeff's path. Trees like great shadows loomed out of the deeper darkness of the storm, and the icy wind gnawed at his face.

A person wouldn't last long out here without shelter.

The notion terrified him. On its heels came the image of Jeff's face, a blue mask of agony, staring with frozen, lifeless eyes.

Matt plodded on, forcing the vision from his head. The outhouse stood only thirty yards from the cabin, but the trek seemed much longer. He grew afraid that Jeff had missed it and wandered off into the storm, but suddenly the tall, narrow building loomed before him. The snow mounted against the dark, weather-worn wood of its walls, striving to reach the thick accumulation on the roof.

Matt swept the beam over the snow. Jeff's path led to the outhouse. No other paths branched out.

"Jeff," he called, raising his voice to match the storm. "Are you still in there?"

The wind moaned through cracks in the old boards. He rubbed his hands together before knocking. "Jeff?"

He grasped the handle. The door creaked, hesitant to open. He shined the flashlight inside, sweeping the beam across the old wooden bench and black plastic toilet seat. He saw no sign of the boy.

Matt slipped into the outhouse, feeling his insides sink. The acrid smell of sewage stung his nostrils, and he shuddered. Fear heightened his need to urinate. He undid his fly and pissed as the wind whispered outside, murmuring darkness.

His heart raced; he reminded himself not to panic.

The wind picked up, a powerful gust that shook the outhouse, rattling the door. He finished urinating and zipped his fly. What the hell was he going to do?

Matt opened the door, pushing hard against the mounting snow. The storm raged on. He shivered, watching the snow cavort in violent circles against a backdrop of darkness, a dance of grace and chaos, its effect mesmerizing.

Dread crawled up his spine as he watched and listened. The

wind's voice changed, splitting into a number of distinct voices that whispered an unnatural chorus in the darkness. The storm felt and sounded unnatural. Matt trembled, and he had the sudden, strong feeling that he was not alone.

"Jeff?"

A scream rose above the voices of the storm, a discordant cry of agony and terror. The sound cut through dark and snow, ringing in his head, driving a chill deep into his soul. He wanted to run, but his legs were rigid, unmoving, as if the storm itself held him in its icy claws.

Suddenly, a light shone to his right. He turned his head, trying to breathe. The windows of the cabin glowed in the twisting snow and darkness. He forced himself towards them, each step a struggle in the heavy drifts. A shadow flitted through the dull yellow light.

"Jeff!" he cried.

The wind's voices faded, ending with a cruel, joyless laugh. His heart pounded, and terror drove him on. He scrambled through the snow, tripping, digging his way forward with his hands. The storm howled all around him. As he neared the cabin, the front door opened, spilling more light into the night.

"Matt? Jeff?" called Tracy.

"Stay inside," he shouted. "Don't come out here."

She stepped out. "Are you guys out there?"

"GET BACK INSIDE!"

She recoiled in fear, her head whipping around. He shined the flashlight in her face. Her eyes opened wide with fear. "Did you hear that scream. Was that you?"

Matt drove himself through a drift to the doorstep. He grabbed her and pulled her inside, slamming the door.

"What's going on?" she demanded, her face flushing.

He let go of her and strode to the fireplace. He took the gun down and opened the barrel.

"Matthew! What the hell are you doing?"

"There's something out there." He hurried into the kitchen,

pulling open a drawer and taking out a box of shells. He slammed them down on the counter. The box burst open, and shells fell clinking to the floor.

"If you guys are trying to scare me . . ."

Matt felt his face redden as he looked at her. "Do you really think I would put this much effort into scaring my pregnant wife?"

Her eyes, narrow and angry, smoothed with worry. "Oh my God, where's Jeff?"

Matt snatched two shells from the counter. His hands shook as he plunked them into the gun. "He's out there."

"Where?" she asked, panicking.

"I don't know," he barked, snapping the gun shut.

"Matt," she said, wounded, "you're scaring me."

He swallowed hard and took a deep breath. "I'm sorry. I'm scared, too. I don't know where he is. He went to the outhouse and I can't find him. He's been gone over an hour and a half."

She looked at the gun. "You're not going back out."

"It's freezing outside. He could die."

The words stunned her. Her mouth hung open, her eyes alight with horror.

"I'm going to try the phone in the truck." He dug into his coat pocket, felt the cold metal of the keys. "If the phone works, I'll try the state police. Maybe they can send a rescue team."

"Should I come with you?"

"No," he snapped. "You stay here."

"What if it's a joke?"

He stopped at the door. "If he's screwing around, I'll shoot him. I swear to God."

Bracing himself for the storm's onslaught, Matt ventured back into the night. His threat aside, he hoped to see a path down to the truck, but he found only unbroken snow below the cabin. He could not see the vehicle through the storm. He took a best guess at its direction, bulling his way through the snow. The chill wind bit his face, and the snowflakes that struck there pierced like needles.

He had worked his way no more than fifteen feet when an unnatural exhaustion set in; the cold leeched strength from his limbs quickly as he struggled forward. His arms ached as he held the gun above the snow. His legs throbbed, and the harsh air stung his lungs.

He almost missed the truck. Snow drifts had mounted to the windows. He set the gun on the roof and dug the door out with his hands, trying to ignore the cold. He climbed in and slammed the door against the storm. The wind removed, he felt warmer. He dug out the keys and tried the ignition. The engine sputtered low, then turned over. He reached down, pushing the gas pedal with his hand, revving the motor. He wondered if they could make it down the hill, even with four-wheel drive.

Shivering, he rubbed his hands together and flipped the heat on. He hit the switch for the dash lights. The cab glowed with eerie, digital-green light. He picked up the car phone and dialed 911. Static crackled in his ear, but the line rang.

"Thank God," he said.

He glanced back toward the cabin. The unseen wind drove snow across the light from the windows, and he saw that the drifts had climbed the walls to the base of glass. His eyes lingered there as a female voice answered.

"Nine-one-one. What is your emergency?"

"I'm at a cabin off of Parker Hollow Road. Our nephew is lost in the storm. We need help."

"Okay, sir. Relax. Give us your exact location."

The cabin lights flickered and grew dim, the light dying on the snow outside.

"Sir? We need your location," she said. "Sir?"

"I . . ." said Matt. He watched in horror as the lights surged bright, then went out. The storm engulfed the cabin in snow and darkness.

The wind's tone changed. He pulled the phone from his ear, listening intently. He heard furtive whispers on the gale outside. Pinpricks of gooseflesh broke out on his arms. His breath quickened, his chest tightening with terror at the malevolent voices of the storm.

"Sir?" came the voice over the phone.

Matt raised it to his ear. "I'll call you back . . ."

He hung up, staring at the dark place where the cabin stood. "Tracy," he said.

The sinister voices carried on, rising in volume and intensity, phantom murmurs of cold and fear. His heart throbbed as he reached for the door handle. She was alone in the dark.

He threw the door open. Leaping out, he tripped, falling face first into the snow. The cold gnawed at his naked skin as he scrambled to his feet. He snatched the gun from the roof. Terror renewed his strength, and he hurried back through the path he had plowed.

As he neared the cabin, he could see dim red light through the windows. The wind's voices grew louder in his head, a haunting cacophony of tortured, malignant cries. He covered his ears to ward them off.

He reached the cabin door. He burst inside and slammed the door shut. He leaned against it, trying to catch his breath. "Tracy?"

She must have put more wood on the fire. It sputtered, burning bright, and the room flickered with its orange glare. The grandfather clock ticked without mercy. "Tracy, where are you?"

"I'm here," she said, her voice weak, frightened. She sat on the floor in the corner near the fireplace, at the base of the clock, her arms drawn around her knees.

Matt rushed to her side. "Are you all right?"

"Do you hear them, Matthew?" she asked, her voice haunted. "Do you hear the voices?" She looked pale, even in the dim firelight. He took her hand. It felt cold, despite the chill in his own.

"I hear them," he said, reassuring.

Her beautiful eyes bulged, obscene with terror. "What is it?"

Trembling, he looked around the cabin. "I don't know."

The wind howled outside. An angry, powerful gust rattled the door and shook the windows. The snow moved in a perfect line from side to side, driven by the wind's wrath. Matt stared in shock, his heart cold and slow. The snow thickened outside, snowflakes ricocheting madly off some unseen presence, creating tenuous, shadowy forms. Dark phantoms emerged, their shapes held by the wild, swirling flakes of snow. The specters had dull, blue pricks of fire on their empty faces, eyes that burned deep in the surrounding darkness.

"Don't move, honey," said Matt. His words were wasted; she stared out the window, eyes wide, body stiff with terror.

Matt walked into the center of the room.

The wind shrieked with vengeance. He heard a roar like the screech of twisted metal, and with a thunderous, rending crack the cabin door burst open.

He raised the gun. It shook in his hands, and his finger trembled on the trigger. He squeezed, firing one shot out the open door, into the heart of the storm. The explosion echoed, driven back into the room by a great gust of wind. A thick wave of snow rode the breeze, swirling inside the cabin.

An unnatural blast of icy air slammed into him, knocking him to the floor. He lay on his back, quaking as he stared in awe.

The snow danced in circles before the door, twisting around, creating a vague shape out of nothingness. Snowflakes flowed into the dark phantom, clinging to its emerging form, vaguely the shape of a large man. Its eyes glowed, burning bright blue on its dark, spectral face.

In the grip of sheer terror, a single thought ran through Matt's mind. His grandfather hadn't told him about the snowmen to scare him.

It had been a warning.

The ghostly blue eyes settled on Matt, and he froze, chilled with the cold of a thousand harsh winters.

The phantom spoke in a low, frigid rasp. "We accept your sacrifice. Your son will be born free." The wind shrieked outside, wicked and gleeful. "We will come to your son's son, in his time, when his wife is ripe with their firstborn."

The snowman turned, focusing its cold stare on Tracy. The couch blocked her from Matt's view, but he heard her terrified whimpering intensify.

The specter gazed back at him. "They will give a suitable offering, else their unborn child will we take."

Matt stuttered, grappling with the terror. He forced the words from his mouth, "Where's Jeff . . ."

The phantom's face remained cold and constant. "We have taken him."

The voices outside rose in faint, twisted laughter. The wind picked up, howling through the cabin. The snowflakes that circled the phantom widened their arc. Its eyes faded as its form unraveled into the swirling snow, which hovered a moment before it flew out the door.

Matt stared in shock out the broken door as the gale lost its fury, hushing to a mournful winter breeze.

The snow continued to fall.

Champion of Lost Causes

by Scott Emerson Bull

Scott Emerson Bull has been weaving creepy tales for seven years now, scribbling them down in an old stone cottage nestled in rural Carroll County, Maryland. His first published story, "Champion of Lost Causes," (Terminal Fright, *Winter '95, reprinted with permission in* Breaking Boundaries) *received an honorable mention in* The Year's Best Fantasy and Horror. *Since then, he has appeared in issues of* Outer Darkness, The Grimoire, Gathering Darkness, Nocturnal Mutterings, *and* White Knuckles.

"Champion of Lost Causes" was written during the time of the O.J. trial and bears that influence somewhat, though the real inspiration was a lawyer that happened to fall in my sphere of acquaintance for a short time. Fictional characters being what they are, this one decided he'd rather have nothing to do with his real-life counterpart and morphed himself into something wholly different. Thank God for that.

Champion of Lost Causes

Some would say logic has no place in law, that lawyers are too pre-occupied with the smoke and mirrors of their trade to navigate the twisting corridors of reason. But F. Thomasen, Esquire took to those narrow passageways with vigor. Inside-out thinking was his passion. He loved nothing more than turning around his opponent's arguments so he could throw them back in their face, which was a good thing considering the surreal horrors committed by some of his clients. Logic was sometimes the only thing that kept his feet rooted to the ground when all around was madness.

But logic was failing him now. He'd spent the last three hours mired in the legal briefs of a man in his late twenties who had mowed down three people on a public thoroughfare with a late model sports car. The man showed no remorse, which made it tough for Thomasen to come up with any sort of credible defense. How did he end up with such scum, he cursed himself. Why couldn't he have followed a more respectable path through the legal system, one leading to rich clientele and the judgeship he'd long ago given up on. Notoriety, that's why. That and the thrill of winning when the odds weighed against you. Damn the clients. They were just props. Pawns in an elaborate chess match. It wasn't them on trial. It was Thomasen. Thomasen the unfeeling bastard. Thomasen the shark. Thomasen who won and almost never lost.

A migraine was fast approaching. The appearance of his secretary at the door of his office brought welcome relief.

"Mr. Thomasen? There's a young woman here to see you. Very pretty. Says she's a lost cause."

"Lost cause, eh?" Thomasen glanced at the photo of his latest lover on the corner of his desk; the gold frame that until recently had held a picture of his wife, another lost cause. "Send her down to Hammonds. Why am I suddenly the champion of lost causes?"

"Mr. Hammonds is in court. Besides, she asked for you personally."

Thomasen eased back into his leather chair and looked at the stack of legal briefs on his desk. Three murders, the aforementioned vehicular homicide, and an assault and battery; all of them coming to trial within the next three months. Make the girl wait for Hammonds, he thought. He'd be a better choice anyway. Hammonds the do-gooder. Hammonds the saint. Hammonds with the principles so damn high he made you want to puke.

"You say she's pretty, huh?"

"Reddish-brown hair. Slim. Twenty, maybe twenty-one."

What the hell, he thought. Thomasen took out a yellow legal pad and a Cross pen. "Send her in."

The girl entered and shyly shook Thomasen's hand. Her touch was smooth, yielding, and her looks confirmed his secretary's assessment and then some. Soft, amber curls fell gently on either side of her face framing high, delicate cheekbones beneath clear, emerald eyes. But beneath her beauty she wore her burdens like a coat too heavy for her shoulders. The weight seemed to pull her down into the chair as Thomasen offered it to her.

"Are you good?" she asked, and for a moment Thomasen wondered whether she was inquiring about his talents as a lawyer or as a lover. "The best," he smiled in answer to both.

"You were the one that got that kid off who slaughtered his parents, weren't you?"

Thomasen offered the girl a cigarette. She refused. "I helped him out. Least I could do. The kid was crazy, but he didn't deserve to fry." He lit himself a cigarette and studied the girl's face.

Something in it struck a distant chord; a memory that defied recall.

"But what he did was terrible," she said. "Didn't he just keep stabbing them over and over?"

"One hundred and thirty-two times, to be exact. With a steak knife."

"And you got him set free."

There was no accusation in her tone, just a simple stating of fact. Thomasen blew out a gust of smoke. "I got him help, which is what he needed. It's not my job to pass moral judgment on my clients. It's my job to get them the best deal I can."

"Will you help me?" she asked.

Thomasen looked again at the briefs on his desk, then back at the face that seemed so familiar. He got out of his chair and walked to the front of his desk, taking a seat on its edge so he could appear more trusting, more supportive.

"That depends," he said.

"Depends?"

Thomasen straightened his silk tie. As he did, his elbow glanced against the marble statue on his desk, causing the scales of justice to wobble.

"Depends on whether you're guilty or not."

"Oh, I'm guilty," she said. "Guilty as sin."

The girl told her story slowly and without emotion, though pain seemed to simmer close beneath the surface. Thomasen scribbled notes on a legal pad.

"It was last Spring. I'd come home early from a date. Mom was away on business, and I told my Dad I'd be spending the night at a girl friend's—that's what I always told him when I planned to sleep with Jeff. Jeff was my boyfriend."

"Go on."

"Jeff and I had a fight, so I ended up going home instead." The girl's voice trailed off and a little of the hurt bubbled to the top. "When I got there I found my father in the living room. He was on the couch with some woman from work. I recognized her from a dinner party my parents had given the week before. I can still see the bitch shoving down my Mom's hors d'oeuvres."

"What were they doing?"

She threw Thomasen an impatient glance. "Use your imagination."

"So what did you do?"

The girl squirmed in the chair, as if it had suddenly grown uncomfortable. "I freaked. I started screaming and running around the room throwing things. The woman got scared and grabbed her clothes and ran for the door. Daddy just kept yelling at me to stop. He grabbed my arms and started shaking me. When that didn't work, he slapped me in the mouth." The girl looked up at Thomasen, blood rising in waves to her face. "He never should have hit me."

Thomasen got up and poured the girl a brandy from the bar. She cupped the glass tightly in both hands, as if warming herself, then downed the liquor in one swallow. She handed the snifter back to Thomasen.

"What happened next?" he asked.

The girl's gaze dropped to her lap, where she was pulling on the fingers of each hand as if making sure they were still firmly attached. "I went to my room and pretended to sleep, while Dad stayed downstairs and drank himself into a stupor. About an hour later, I heard him stumble upstairs to bed.

"When I was sure he was asleep, I went down to the basement and got some fishing line: the real strong kind my dad used when he'd go out on the ocean. I brought it upstairs and tied one end of it around the brass rail in the headboard of his bed. Then I took the other end and tied it around his throat."

"He didn't feel anything?"

She pulled hard on the thumb of her left hand. "The bastard snored the whole time."

The girl got out of her seat and walked to the window. She

stood there for a moment, silently looking out at the street below, then resumed her story.

"After I secured the fishing line, I went down to the kitchen and got the evening paper and a pack of matches. They were both lying on the table where he usually left them." She turned and sort of half-smiled. "I always told father he should give up smoking."

Thomasen coughed and stubbed out his cigarette.

"I went back upstairs, rolled up the newspaper, and lit the end. Then I held the paper up to the smoke detector outside my father's bedroom. When the smoke detector went off, Daddy shot straight up in bed. The police said if it hadn't been for the bones in his neck, the fishing line would have gone all the way through."

Thomasen dropped the pen on his desk.

"You're Lisa Jacobson."

The girl nodded.

"But they ruled your father's death a suicide. They found a note on his computer."

"I typed it," she said coolly.

Thomasen poured himself a whiskey and joined the girl at the window. She had looked so young on television, dressed in funereal black with her hair pulled into loose braids. The story at the time was that Lisa had found her father hanging from the chandelier above his bed. She said she had cut him down because she couldn't bear to see his body swing back and forth. No one had ever suspected foul play. Most people, it seemed, were just happy to be rid of the guy.

"Look, Lisa. You're a free woman. Are you sure you want to confess?"

Lisa turned towards Thomasen, a hint of the anger that had killed her father flashing through her eyes. "Confess? I don't want to confess! I feel no guilt at all over what I've done. My father was a bastard."

"Then why do you need my help?"

Lisa looked back out the window. "My father was not wealthy

by accident, Mr. Thomasen. I'm sure you heard all about the indictments and the investigations. But they could never pin anything on him, could they? He had protection. Certain people with whom he'd made *arrangements* to insure his success. People for whom he would do certain favors."

Lisa's hands were trembling. Thomasen poured her another brandy.

"I was aware that his wealth was, shall we say, tainted," he said. "But I never knew he was involved with the underworld. He didn't seem the type."

Lisa wrapped her arms around herself, as if trying to stave off a chill. "They know everything about what happened. I don't know how, but they just know. They want me to stand before them and answer for my crime." She turned her eyes to Thomasen. "I need you to help me plead my case."

Thomasen ran a hand through his thin, graying hair. He'd had one or two brushes with the underworld in the past and been fortunate to come away unbloodied. He didn't relish another encounter, but the idea of pleading a case in front of a merciless court appealed to him. And like any lawyer smelling a challenge, he thought he could win.

"This is most unusual, Miss Jacobson. I generally work in a court of law."

"Name your price," she said.

"Money's not really the issue."

Lisa looked at him with misting eyes. She pulled on a lock of hair, twisting it around her finger. As she did, the years seemed to melt from her. She could have been sixteen.

"When will you need my help?" he asked.

"They're sending a car," she said, pointing out the window. "In fact, it looks like they're here now."

The black limo was waiting for them at the curb, the smoke from its exhaust giving it an ethereal quality as it swirled around the car and reflected in its black tinted windows. The sun was sneaking behind the office block, and Thomasen felt the damp night seep into his bones. He had a sudden urge to go back and get his gun, but decided against it. They'd find it for sure, and probably use it to shoot them both.

"I'll follow you in my car," he said.

"No way," Lisa said. "They'll never go for that!"

The rear door of the limo opened. Thomasen looked inside, expecting someone to step out. The back seat was empty.

"Let's go," she said.

They huddled into the back seat, easing into worn pockets in the scarred leather. There was a gaping hole with a few bare wires where the television had once been, and the brass mini-bar, now tarnished green, was devoid of alcohol. Cheap bastards, Thomasen thought. Least they could do was let you have a drink. He pulled the door shut, and the limo lurched forward into the street.

Lisa had grown visibly more nervous.

"You won't tell them I was temporarily insane, will you?" she asked. "Like that kid?"

"Possibly. It's a good defense."

"They'll laugh at you," she said.

They sped down Perring Parkway into the City, then took a confusing array of side streets until they entered a section of town littered with failed businesses and shuttered warehouses. An area that seemed to have resigned itself to its blight, giving refuge to the crack dealers and other low-lifes that slipped amongst its shadows. Out of habit, Thomasen looked to see if he recognized anyone he might have once represented.

"I'm going to lose, aren't I?" she said.

Thomasen looked over at her. She was pulling her fingers again and seemed to be shaking. He put an arm around her and pulled her close to comfort her. "Don't worry," he said. "I've haven't lost a client yet." Then he pulled her a little closer, to comfort himself.

The limo turned into a narrow alleyway with tall, brick walls stretching up on either side. After about a hundred yards, they came to a halt in front of a deserted warehouse with gang slogans spray-painted on the walls, their fluorescent letters distorted and dripping, as if written in the very blood of the inner city. Torn bags of trash lay like dead bodies on either side of a metal door that seemed to be the only entrance into the building. Thomasen could smell the stench without getting out of the car.

"This is it," Lisa said.

They exited the relative safety of the limo and stepped onto the grimy tarmac. There was a feeling of hopelessness in the air; the breath of desperation. Thomasen tried the metal door and it opened easily. As they stepped inside, he heard the scurry of tiny claws on the concrete floor. Rats, he thought. Lovely. They entered a dark hallway that led to an even darker staircase and began their descent into hell.

"You act like you've been here before," he said.

"Once. In a nightmare."

They descended six, long flights of stairs before they came to a soot-covered corridor lined with heavy steel pipes and lit by an occasional naked bulb hung from wire. The sound of machinery droned around them, and the air was hot and tasted metallic. Thomasen's pulse quickened. The farther he moved into his opponent's realm, the less control he felt over the situation, and the more he questioned his sanity for taking the case.

A door stood at the end of the corridor. Thomasen turned to point it out to Lisa, when something soft squirmed under his foot. His feet went out from under him and he grabbed one of the pipes, struggling for balance, but heat seared his hands and he fell backwards against the other wall, his head hitting the solitary bulb lighting this end of the tunnel. Shards of glass rained over him, and they were plunged into darkness. Thomasen bit his tongue to stop his scream.

"Are you okay?"

Lisa's hands were in his, helping him up, then her arms were around him, holding him tight. He strained to see in the fathomless dark, but his eyes refused to adjust. For a moment, he felt like running; groping his way back through the dark corridors to the safety of the street. But Lisa's trembling body stopped him. He couldn't desert her, and besides, he had a trial to win. A set of rusty hinges groaned like the foreshadowing of another world, and dim light broke the gloom of the corridor. The door had opened. They were being welcomed inside.

"Come," a tortured voice said, and they followed a shadowy figure into a make-shift courtroom lit by candles and acetylene lamps. The air reeked with the thick odor of human waste and decay, and as Thomasen inspected the crowd in the gallery, he saw why. They were a slovenly collection of derelicts and bag ladies; lost souls only a few steps shy of death. Closely they studied Thomasen and the girl. Already they were making their judgments.

"Jesus," Thomasen whispered. "What the hell is this?"

They were led to a rotting bench in the back; Thomasen wanted to raise his feet in fear of what might run over them. A gavel cracked, and court was brought back to order.

In the dim light, Thomasen saw a young black man standing in the middle of a circle drawn crudely in chalk. In front of him was a large metal grate with hinges, a forbidding door leading to dark depths below. Behind him stood two bailiffs: powerfully built men who seemed somehow out of kilter. Perhaps it was the way their shoulders hunched and deformed beneath their grimy, blue uniforms. Or the way their heads seemed too big for their bodies. In front of this trio stood a simple metal desk—the judge's bench—and behind it sat the judge himself, his features hidden in shadows.

"Have you anything more to say in your pathetic defense?" he asked.

"Please," the black man pleaded, his voice quivering like a

thin reed in a gale. "I couldn't help myself. There was just so much money. I couldn't resist. Please spare me!"

The judge laughed: a foul, horrible laugh that was echoed by the filth in the gallery. "Did you really think we wouldn't find out? We told you we have eyes everywhere. It was your misfortune to doubt that."

The man was weeping. Thomasen hated that sort of show of emotion in a man. He wanted to tell the guy to pull himself together and accept his consequences with dignity. Anyone could see that groveling would bring no mercy in this court. But Thomasen remained seated, and to his disgust, the man fell to his knees. He placed the palms of his hands together and prayed to the judge.

"I beg you. Please don't . . . ."

Out of the shadows, the judge's hand appeared, stark white flesh against the black of his robe. He chose a quill pen from a selection on his desk and dipped it into a well of ink. With a long, bony finger, he traced along the names in the ledger open before him. Finding the one he wanted, he made a check mark with the bold sweep of his hand. "I hereby find you guilty as charged. Punishment will be immediate."

Again the gavel fell with a crack. The judge leaned forward out of the shadows, and Thomasen got the first glimpse of his opponent. The view made him cringe. The man's hair was matted and black, and in the dim light seemed to squirm, like worms waiting to become bait. His skin was pallid and pulled too tight against his bones, giving him the appearance of Death, or at least one of its servants. His eyes were closed, and Thomasen saw from the red welts of flesh that his eyelids had been cauterized shut. Justice was, indeed, blind.

"Jesus, Lisa. What the hell are these things?"

Her voice came in spasms. "Daddy called them the demons of greed. It wasn't until they came to accuse me, that I realized what he'd meant."

Thomasen looked back at the chalk circle and the trembling

black man. He'd expected the bailiffs to lead the man away, but to his confusion they each took two steps backward. From beneath the floor there was a grinding of metal and the grate opened to reveal crumbling concrete steps leading into utter darkness. The black man raised his eyes to a heaven far removed from the squalid hell they were in now, as if beseeching a god that had already deserted him. Then, in a dim flash of light, four chains rose from the steps like arms groping blindly in the dark. They seemed to be working of their own volition, for Thomasen could see no apparatus or person manipulating them. They hovered for a second, like the tentacles of some horrible octopus, and he saw that each chain held a large, blackened, meat hook. There was a dull clang as the links in the chains snapped like a steel whip and the hooks found purchase in the man's body: two ripping into his chest; two in his back.

Screams of terror pierced through Thomasen. He covered his ears, but there was no denying the cries of pain. Around him, the gallery of vagrants murmured appreciatively, scuttling forward on their seats to better their view. Thomasen closed his eyes and waited for the shrieking to stop. When it finally had, he looked back to where the man had stood. The circle was empty, and the gate leading to unknown horrors below was closed.

Lisa shook uncontrollably, her breath coming in panicked sobs. He put his arm around her to comfort her, but it did little good. The futility of their situation—of arguing a case in front of these bloodthirsty demons—was readily apparent. Thomasen formulated a plan of escape. The bailiffs had not yet come for them; the big men were waiting, presumably, for the judge's order. If they made a run for it now, they might reach safety.

"Come on," he whispered to Lisa. "Let's get the hell out of here."

But Lisa wouldn't budge. "No."

"Come on," Thomasen said, his own voice now quivering. "We can make it!"

"You don't understand. There's no use in running. They'll find me. There's no escape."

And now it was too late. The bailiffs were standing over them, their faces expressionless, their skin slack, like costume masks that didn't quite fit. Their eyes burned black with an intelligence that didn't appear human.

From behind them, the judge's voice boomed.

"Will Miss Jacobson please appear before the court."

"No escape," she repeated.

Led by the bailiffs, they approached the bench: Lisa going inside the circle of chalk; Thomasen standing just off to her right.

The judge looked up from his ledger. "I see you've brought a friend with you," he said. "And who might this be?"

"I'm Miss Jacobson's lawyer," Thomasen said. "I'm here to see she gets a fair trial."

"A lawyer," the judge said, raising his sightless eyes. "How interesting."

Thomasen approached the bench, searching deep inside, hoping to find his nerve. "Your honor," he said, adopting his trial voice. "I thought we might start by reviewing the facts."

"Don't speak to me of facts, Mr. Thomasen," the judge sneered. "Lawyers deal in perceptions, not truths. And you will find that this court is not as naive as the ones you've practiced in before."

Stay loose, he told himself. Don't let him shake you. Forget the horrors you've just seen. Forget the man's eyes. "My apologies, your honor. It was not my intent to insult the court."

"Good. See that it doesn't happen again." The judge smiled. "My patience is rather short today."

Thomasen sucked in a deep breath and called up the actor from within. He would need all his powers of persuasion just to have a chance of winning this one. He only hoped the tricks of psychology that worked so well on humans, would work on this thing in front of him.

"I believe, your honor," he began, "that we need to examine

who is the true victim here. Is it Mr. Jacobson? Or is it his daughter?"

The judge laughed, and again the gallery joined in. "Oh, Lord," he said to no one in particular. "He's going to have her plead insanity? How trite!"

"No, sir," Thomasen said, feeling his adrenaline flow. "I am not."

"Then what is your point?"

Thomasen turned to the gallery and looked at the drawn faces smeared black with grime and despair. They looked at him suspiciously, as if they wanted him to get on with it, so they could see another killing.

"The facts are indisputable. Miss Jacobson did kill her father, which she freely admits. And the ingenuity of her method leads one to believe that she was of a balanced mind when she committed the crime. She was not acting out of impulse."

"That is the belief of this court," the judge said.

"But is there not a certain amount of justice in her crime? Did not Mr. Jacobson deserve the end he received?"

The judge pushed aside his ledger and scratched at the wound on his right eyelid.

"And if I might be so bold, your honor," Thomasen went on. "It would not surprise me if Mr. Jacobson's name was in your ledger, and that perhaps Miss Jacobson saved you a little effort."

Again the judged smiled. Thomasen wasn't sure whether the rat's maze of teeth meant the judge was enjoying the battle of wits, or simply amused at Thomasen's feeble defense. "The contents of this book are no concern of yours, Mr. Thomasen. Though I will grant you, Mr. Jacobson might well have been a worthy addition."

Score one for our side, he thought. He turned to Lisa to give her a reassuring smile, but her eyes were blank. She looked as if she wasn't even there.

"However," the judge went on. "Mr. Jacobson should have had the opportunity to plead his case. Been given, to use your own words, a fair trial. It's true he was guilty of some of the most appalling sins, most of which Miss Jacobson is wholly unaware, but it was not within her authority to play judge and executioner."

"But then that is her only crime," Thomasen snapped, turning back to the bench. "She stepped over the bounds of her authority."

"Authority," the judged howled. "She has no authority!"

"But she does, your honor. As members of society we all have the authority to make moral judgments. The right to ostracize those we feel have broken certain moral codes."

The judge leaned forward in his chair. "But does not your Bible say, 'Judge not, lest ye be judged.' Or are you unfamiliar with the work?"

Thomasen fussed with his tie and the buttons on his double-breasted suit—a sure sign that logic was failing him. He never fared well when he was put on the defensive. Thomasen always did better when he came out with both guns blaring. From the time he'd entered the limo, his opponents had claimed the upper hand. And now he felt the corner he'd been backed into closing around him.

He set his jaw and continued. "But the use of ordinary citizens to pass judgment—the right to be judged by a jury of our peers—is the very cornerstone of our justice system. Miss Jacobson was well qualified to judge her father's actions. And if we look at his crimes, was not Mr. Jacobson's death warranted? Even justified?"

The judge shook his head. "If the scope of all his crimes were taken together, yes. But she knew of only one crime, and death is hardly fair punishment for marital infidelity." The judge leaned forward again and cleared his throat. "And considering your past, Mr. Thomasen, you better hope it isn't."

Thomasen felt his nerve slipping and tried to wrench it back. "Agreed. The punishment did not fit the crime. Just as the punishment of death does not fit Miss Jacobson's crime."

The judge straightened and began sifting through his assortment of quill pens. "Her crime is murder, Mr. Thomasen," the judge said, sounding suddenly bored, "and the punishment for murder is death. There are no degrees in murder, just as there are no degrees in death. Miss Jacobson's fate is clear."

"But, you honor . . ."

"I've entertained your arguments for long enough, Mr. Thomasen. Man needs to begin taking responsibility for his crimes, not look for excuses as to why they should be pardoned. But then that would put an awful lot of your type out of work wouldn't it?"

Thomasen now knew why the black man had begged. Eventually, it became the only option. "But justice must be fair," Thomasen pleaded. "It must consider all the circumstances surrounding a crime."

"Enough!" the judge said. From beneath the floor, Thomasen heard the grind of metal. Chains being coiled.

"But your honor!"

The judge ignored him and opened the ledger. He wet his pen with ink and made another check mark.

"Guilty as charged."

Lisa sobbed into her hands. Thomasen went to console her, but one of the misshapen bailiffs pushed him away. He turned back to the judge, who seemed smug in his victory. He fought the compulsion to drop to his knees.

"Your honor, I beg you . . . ."

The judge raised his hand for Thomasen to be quiet. In the ensuing silence, Thomasen searched hard inside for some method of bartering Lisa out of certain death. He couldn't bear the thought of losing this case. He needed to make a deal, a plea bargain, anything. Just then, the hardness of the judge's face seemed to soften, as if he had been reading Thomasen's mind.

"I will agree to stay punishment, Mr. Thomasen, if councilor agrees to certain terms."

Thomasen approached the bench. "Yes, your honor?"

"As a lawyer, what is your duty to your client?"

He answered without hesitation. "To get them the best deal possible."

"At any price?"

"At any price."

The judge smiled through his rotted teeth.

"Mr. Thomasen, I will agree to let Miss Jacobson go free on the condition that you take her place in the circle."

Thomasen stepped back from the bench. The chains rattled below, as if in anticipation.

"But your honor . . . ."

"Do you not understand the terms?"

"Yes, but . . . ."

"Then the court wishes your answer, Mr. Thomasen. Yes or no?"

Thomasen looked at Lisa. Her body was hunched and weary, her eyes bloodshot from crying. The grinding beneath the floor grew louder, joined by a whirring sound, like metal points being sharpened.

"But . . . ."

"Your answer, Mr. Thomasen."

In his mind, Thomasen kneeled before the gods of logic, as blood pounded through his veins. He felt the gallery reaching for him, their clothes hanging in strips from emaciated arms and hands. In his mind, he saw the chains snap and rip through his flesh. He saw the judge's eyelids tearing open so they could enjoy the show.

"Your answer!"

"Wait!" Thomasen scrambled towards the bench. The adrenaline was back, the fight returning to his body. "Maybe there's another way."

"My patience is at an end, Mr. Thomasen."

"But I have a better answer. One that will benefit us both."

"I'm listening."

Thomasen took a deep breath. "Wouldn't I be worth more

alive? Wouldn't a lawyer of my talents be better used in your service?"

The judge rose from behind his desk. The rattling of chains ceased, at least for the moment.

"You wish to bargain with us?"

"Yes."

The judge approached him, moving confidently in spite of his blindness. "But how do you know we can be trusted to keep our end of the bargain?"

"What choice do I have?"

"You can leave," the judge said, his body now close enough for Thomasen to take in its sour stench. "Walk away. Let the bitch die! We've no quarrel with you. You'll never hear from us again."

Thomasen looked straight into the judge's scarred eyelids. "I can't. I've never lost a client to the death penalty and I'm not going to lose one to you. There's always a way out, even if it's life without parole." Thomasen forced a smile. "And I always find that way out."

The judge smiled. The reek of a thousand executions seeped from his mouth.

"I admire your arrogance. But I wonder if such an ego would not be wasted on a lawyer. I can imagine you as an equal. As a peer."

The judge put his hands on Thomasen's shoulders, and Thomasen felt his knees weaken and his boughs loosen. But he refused to let his eyes waver from those horrid sockets. Not now, he told himself. Not when victory was so close at hand.

Then the judge gave his verdict.

"Let the bitch go," he said.

Thomasen heard the scuffle of feet as Lisa stumbled from the circle. Heard her cries as she pushed through the crowd towards the door, their grimy hands pawing at her body. They seemed reluctant to let go of such an appetizing sacrifice.

"The deal is made," the judge said, and Thomasen was aware

of the thing's grip tightening on his shoulders. The bailiff's had moved closer, blocking any escape. "You will be a judge, Thomasen. You will preside over the highest authority, letting vent to your deepest desires of power. The masses will bow to you, slave to you, but you will be *ours*."

Thomasen felt the room spin, but beneath his nausea, adrenaline surged, rekindling the embers of a dream long died out. As judge, Thomasen would no longer be forced to play the game. He would be the game. He would be the one calling the shots, determining who won and lost. They'd all bow to him. They'd all be kissing ass.

"Prepare, Thomasen, to receive your dream."

His knees gave out as the two bailiff's grabbed his arms.

"Receive your dream."

The judge placed his thumbs over the sockets of Thomasen's eyes. His mind became a blur of images. Images of victims stumbling past, their bodies hacked and mangled, just as they had appeared in countless crime scene photographs. Victims of the monsters Thomasen had so diligently worked to set free, or at least spare death.

"Receive your dream."

Thomasen fought to escape, but the bailiffs gripped harder, and the judge increased his pressure. He felt a sharp burning on his eyelids and smelled the raw sourness of cooked flesh, as he realized over which court he was to preside. Logic had betrayed him. Logic had doubled back and bitten him hard on the ass. As his consciousness waned, he saw the foul worshipping masses prostrate at his feet and saw the chains snap under his command. Saw them through eyes that could not see. The blind eyes of justice.

Cairns

by Suzanne Parker

Originally from Alabama, Suzanne lives in the Pacific Northwest with her husband Loren, her dog, Foamy, and her cat, Isis. She greatly misses the Deep South.

Cairns

Prologue: About thirty years ago, Ezekiel Pounder bought himself the most beautiful parcel of land in the state. He got the ground at a fine bargain—being a lifelong cheapskate means that he was born a good haggler when it comes to settling the prices of things. Acreage was relatively inexpensive in those days, and abundant. Ezekiel's ground encompassed a lovely valley bounded by rolling hills, well-drained and blessed with fragrant piney woods, fruit blossoms (including a cherry orchard where the trees stood in rows like soldiers), and a healthy stock of hardwoods whose leaves turned into a riot of red and gold come autumn. Never married, he kept his pastoral paradise to himself and tirelessly discouraged all trespassers, often at gunpoint, until he was finally left there in solitude as he wished. I was one of the very few fortunates he allowed to set foot upon his soil—and one was not permitted to wander without his escort.

I live in town, making my trade as a stone mason and carver as I always have. Ezekiel and I go back forever; we were boys together at the local school, which was long-closed as the children grew up and moved away while no one settled in to take their place. There are only a few of us old people now, and I suppose the town will finally die out when we do.

Ezekiel's tombstone has been my project for the past several years, even though he is a cheapskate and will never pay what the stone is worth. I think his yearning for a fine monument was born in our boyhood: We would read books on the tombs of Egypt and look at pictures of the sandstone marvels—later we graduated to the pristine marbles of ancient Greece and Rome. We spent untold hours walking in the old Pisgah Cemetery, climbing the sharp wrought-iron fence that surrounded the graves like a stand of spears, studying the shapes and reading the verse on the markers, taking pencil and paper etchings of their poignant words: "Gone But Not Forgotten", "Asleep in Jesus", "Into Thy Hands I Commend My Spirit", and the popular but—in our opinion—pedestrian "Rest In Peace." We cultivated an early interest in the mortality of earthly things as we sat on the stone benches and ate our sack lunches, facing the carved words "Taken From Us Too Soon." Fascinated, I started whittling on pieces of wood. My course was set when Ezekiel and I found a mysterious golden rock that clanged rather than clunked when we dropped it on the cobbled road. I was determined to uncover the secret of it, and while Ezekiel was adamant that we use the flattened belly of the rock to crush insects with, I couldn't rest until I had vetoed him and swiped a ballpean hammer to split the rock with. I struck the stone again and again even as it rang out its protest, knowing I could learn more from its innards than by handling it intact. Determination and an arm strengthened from a summer of baseball finally won out and the rock broke open for me: we suddenly looked like a pair of skinny young birds, flapping our arms to dispel the dusty gray cloud billowing around us when the rock yielded. We were amazed to discover that the apparent sandstone surface hid a hollow core of iron ore that had somehow filled at its formation with an ash-like powder. My love for stone bloomed into raging passion at that very moment, and—right then and there—I dedicated my life to bringing forth the secrets of stones, to finding the beauty and mystery hidden inside them. My dalliance with whittling wood alchemized into the true abiding love of carving rock, and I discovered I could coax a cohort of angels out of a slab of marble, the menagerie of Eden itself from a hunk of granite and into the light of the sun.

This stone for Ezekiel will be my masterpiece. I've carved thousands of markers for others; people from all over the world ask me to bring life to places of death. They have to come to me well in advance of their passing, though: I can't be hurried in this process. Every piece of stone is different; each must be chosen by sight, by feel, by the very soul of it. When I go to the quarries, I ask to be left alone with the silent, unformed blocks— then I stretch my body out along each stone, hugging it with my arms wrapped as far around it as I can reach. I press my face against the rough-hewn surface, testing its purity and hardness. I have a light I wear hooked onto my cap over my eye that I might study the razored slashes of color in marble and the flecks of dark beauty in granite, gazing at it to decide what I will bring forth of it. I won't presume to call myself an artist; rich people have asked to me to carve statues for their gardens and houses, but I only create markers. If they want my carving, they can buy a tombstone. But they'd better not try to tell me how to carve it— the stone tells me how it wants to be carved.

As Ezekiel and I grew older, each of us followed his own path to true love. My destination was named Nora, and she loved flowering plants as I worshipped stone. Her wreathes and casket covers were beautiful beyond words, and we were the perfect team for most of the years of my life. Now that she has departed, I've mostly retired. The stones and I both miss her. I work on Ezekiel's marker on days when I feel like it—'Zeke complains at me to hurry, but I figure he's got awhile left in him—no matter what his doctors say. Ezekiel's lifelong passion hasn't dimmed over the decades and he is still at it.

I never knew anyone to hate vermin and love wet work as much as Ezekiel does. If it can crawl, he can kill it. He loathes bugs and bats, rats and roaches, squirrels and silverfish with a zealot's absolute prejudice. His expertise with pesticides and traps is unmatched, and it made him a rich man at a young age (although to hear him speak of it, he is mired deep in poverty and barely subsisting above starvation). But Ezekiel doesn't do it just for the money; he has obliterated many an infestation for charity over the years. I think I first noticed it during our squabble over the splitting of the wondrous powder rock—he saw only the lethal potential of a heavy flat surface. While some may say that it is typical for boys to pull the wings off flies or burn ants with a magnifying glass, Ezekiel never delighted in torture: He wanted the nuisance du jour dead as quickly as possible in order to move swiftly onto the next nest of vermin. People have commented about how nice it is to live in this area of the county: Picnics can be held on the ground without being invaded by ants, our dogs are blissfully free of ticks and fleas, and no horseflies buzz around to torment the local livestock. I am certain this is Ezekiel's handiwork. He never found his life mate as I did in Nora, but he has kept himself constantly busy because there are always more pests to eradicate.

He finds me working on his tombstone this morning when he stops his car by my masonry, and gets out to give me a Styrofoam cup filled to the brim with steaming coffee. The coffee is strong and foul, much like his temper, and he's in his usual bellicose mood today, frowning as he passes his gimlet eye over the latest testament to my genius with stone. "I like it better with the lambs laying down instead of standing up. Why did you carve them grazing like that? Sheep are stupid, but not stupid enough to try to eat grass off a bare stone."

I feel cranky, too, and knock the little granite ewe off with one well-placed pop of the wedge and chisel.

"Hey—what'd you do that for??!!!!" Maybe he doesn't like the sheep, but 'Zeke can't bear to see his stone desecrated. It adds to the cost.

"You're too old for lambs."

"It's *my* stone and I'll have whatever I want on it. Start over with another lamb."

"Maybe I'll do cherubs . . . "

"No, you won't!" Ezekiel roars. "I want a whole flock of little lambs cavorting across my headstone!"

"What if I just engrave them in relief like this?" I quickly make a rough intaglio of sheep marching in an arc above his name. "I can refine the images later."

"Hmmmmmmmm."

He stands and watches me work for a few minutes. Finally he asks: "Why don't you come over and split a bottle of good whiskey with me tonight?"

"I promised Nora I wouldn't start drinking again once she was gone."

"Well, what about coffee?"

"Keeps me up all night—my kidneys won't take caffeine anymore."

"You got more ailments than a living man can stand. How come you aren't dead by now?"

I laugh. "I have to work on your stone, 'Zeke. Once I set it in place by your head, I can rest. No more alcohol or coffee, but I can have some of that decaffeinated stuff."

"Then I'll have to go to the store," he snorts. "Your problem is that you've never had enough vice in your life."

"We can watch the football game on television—get a listing on who's playing!" I call after him as he backs his car out of my drive. I know well that Ezekiel has little interest in anything except tending his land and exterminating the relentless hordes of vermin.

It's a shame to drive to Ezekiel's house in the dark and miss seeing the beauty of his land. He doesn't believe in spending money on outdoor lighting for his property, either; he sees it during the day and that's enough for him. With my car windows open, I can hear the gentle songs of the crickets, frogs, and night birds. I know he has landscaped his acreage to perfection; as I round a bend, I seem to remember his building a rock waterfall, and listen for the sound of falling water. When I don't hear it, I remember there has been something of a drought this year; the stream feeding the waterfall may be dried up to a trickle after the long summer.

My old friend's home isn't much to look at. Little more than an unpainted shack, most of the space in it is taken up by Ezekiel's laboratory, where he also sleeps on a cot and prepares his meals. Over the years, he has invented pesticides and poisons unknown to the rest of the world—all the better to eradicate the vermin with. I used to urge him to get patents on his formulas, but he always answered me with only the statement, "They're mine," and he would never share or sell them.

Ezekiel meets me at the door, wearing his exterminator's coveralls and a pair of old leather house shoes, eating dry cold cereal out of a big Pyrex beaker. "Want some Crunchy Sugar Bombs?" he asks.

"No, thanks. My diabetes doesn't let me have the sweet stuff anymore."

"Your ailments don't let you do anything. It's a wonder Nora didn't just poison you to put you out of your misery and stop your whining."

"I was healthy as a horse before I got married."

"Then maybe you should've poisoned her."

I pour myself a bowl of Crunchy Sugar Bombs. "Got any milk?"

"I think it's spoiled. There's some bottled water you can pour over it."

"No thanks—I'll eat it dry the way you're eating yours." We sit down on the old barstools by the lab tables. "So what is it you want, 'Zeke?"

He points to the window behind me. "See that?"

I carry my bowl to the window and look out. "See what?"

"The tree stump by the fence. Look at that big old raccoon sitting on the stump, fixing me with its eyes."

"Probably looking for some bugs for dinner. Since when did

you get scared of 'coons, 'Zeke? Think that fat fellow over there is out to get you for killing his Aunt Bertha?"

"Maybe." Ezekiel puts his spoon down and starts eating the cereal with his fingers.

"Why don't you just set out some strychnine for him like you always do when you've got critters?"

"Because he isn't just a 'critter'," Ezekiel says. Suddenly he jumps up and runs past me, stamping hard on the floor as he goes. "Look at this."

"You just killed a cockroach. So what?"

"Cockroaches—in *my* house??!!"

"You're slipping in your old age, that's all. Everybody slows down eventually; it's nothing to get your shorts in a bunch over. Your doctor told you not to get yourself excited—remember?"

"My doctor can go hang himself. I've only got a few days left, and I'll spend them as I please."

Well, heaven forbid I should suggest to Ezekiel that he ignore his bilious nature for once and give himself a few more hours of existence. When I don't answer, he grabs his flashlight and a jacket. "I want you to come and look at something."

We walk into the woods, our way lit only by the bobbing light in his hand. He's marching like a drill sergeant, and trying to keep up with him sets off my emphysema. I have to stop and use the inhaler I always carry in my back pocket. "You act too healthy for a dying man," I gasp when I can find breath enough for my voice.

"One of the joys of dying fast like I am instead of slow like you are. The aches and shakes can't catch up with you as easily when you're always a few steps ahead of them. Now come on— we don't have all night for you to sit around, wheezing and spitting in my piney woods. You're getting that green crud in your lungs all over the expensive Oregon moss I set out last year."

"Sorry."

"Huh." He stalks on ahead of me, making me have to run to

stay even with him. We go deeper into the well-groomed forest. I should have remembered to bring my own flashlight.

Finally he stops and stands his ground just over a small hillock. I know better than to think he's waiting for me to catch up. When I join him, he plays the light ahead into the wooded darkness. "See that?"

"What?"

"The cairn." He gestures with the light over a narrow pile of gray stones about three feet high. It's been here awhile; wood spiders have spun layers upon layers of thick white cobwebs in the spaces between the stones, and the webs are clogged with forest debris. I go forward and touch one of the stones; its stability and soft edges tell me the cairn has stood for several decades—and is composed of very poor-quality stone.

"Who put this up, 'Zeke?"

"Shut up and come on. We have to hurry."

We find many more cairns—about sixty in all—some new, some old—all ranging from two to three feet high and almost as wide as they are tall. When we go back to the house, 'Zeke turns to me and says, "Some vermin won't stay dead."

"Taking trophies now?" I don't like the sound of my own laughter in the darkness.

"Disposing of the carcasses." Then he stops and stands a moment, looking before him into the woods. "All right, all right—stop your yammering."

"You talking to me?"

"If you'd close your trap, then maybe you'd hear 'em, too. Even better, you could try getting your head out of your skull and quit that internal rhapsodizing over your rock collection for awhile."

He turns on his heel and storms off back to his house, with me scurrying behind him to try to keep up with our sole source of light. The screen door slams in my face when I reach it.

Ezekiel rummages around in a potato bin and comes up with

a hammer, which he sets on the kitchenette counter. There are marbly yellow lights in his eyes. "Remember this?"

'Can't say that I do."

"We opened the rock with it—back when we were boys reading about tombs and caves." He picks it up and lovingly turns it over in his hands. "And all the rock's secrets came out. Then, when we were in Sunday school class, we read about Moses striking the stone and water came forth of it. And I wondered: Could I apply these discoveries to my own work?"

He takes the hammer and slams it onto the counter, shattering the Formica. "The principle is simplicity itself. You break something open, and something different comes out. You break a rock and a cloud comes out. You squash a bug and guts come out. You crack a skull, though, and the brain comes out. Life comes out. If varmints had souls—well, I guess they'd come out, too."

"What have you been doing with yourself, 'Zeke?"

"Killing vermin. Vermin of all kinds. I go into the cities to clean up their pestilence, but I never can get all of them out of the nest—they breed like rats, and five come to take the place of the one you just killed. They're so easy, just like squirrels or raccoons—they can't fly off like bats in an attic once you cut a hole in the roof, and they flock to the right bait. I go in at night with my truck, find them in alleyways and under bridges. I used to tell them I had food in my truck, but they aren't interested in food anymore like they were even a few years ago. They want whiskey or drugs nowadays. So I tell them I have what they want—that's the bait. Then they come over to my truck, sniffing for it like mice. Once they lean in or crawl into my truck looking for the bait, I reach into my coveralls pocket, pull out our old ballpean hammer, and bash their brains out. Then I shove the carcass into the back of my truck where I've put down a plastic tarpaulin, bring it back home, and bury it to get rid of it. Nice and neat. It's the only way to do a clean-out, dispose of the remains, and get some free fertilizer into the bargain."

I sit still and listen. I have been his best friend for life, and now—as death finally approaches for both of us, I realize that I never knew him at all. Probably because I didn't want to. My first impulse is to call the police, but I know I can't do that. The years have made us brothers—besides, he has only a few days left in him. His skin and the whites of his eyes are a dreadful yellow, and the meat on his bones has shriveled like parchment.

"I need you to do something for me."

I had stopped listening to his ranting—now I just look at him, unable to speak for the moment.

"It's just like you've always done," he says, exasperated with me. "I wanted to be like you and bring out the secrets buried inside something. But I never could do it, and now I know it's because there never was anything to find in the first place. At first, I only killed insects and animals, and it was always the same—nothing but shiny warm guts in them. I saw you bring beautiful things out of stone, but there's nothing beautiful in vermin; there's nothing for it but to get rid of them. I went on from the six and eight-legged pests with hard shells on their backs to the four-legged, fur-bearing kind, but it was still the same. So I graduated to the two-legged pests. They swarm in the city, and I eradicate them where I find them. And you know what? Busting open a skull is just like pulling the cover off a bucket of slugs."

My mind is reeling; it has suddenly become airless and hot in here. "Are you in trouble with the law?"

"Nope. Nobody even bothers to look for them. Nobody knows who or where they are. Nobody cares. Nameless, pathetic vermin. But they've lately taken to bothering me—now that I'm weak with disease and old age. You'd think they'd have some common courtesy."

"All of this is just your conscience—you finally developed one after all these years."

"Wish it *was* just my conscience. Take a gander around you— now that you know what to look for."

And then I see them. Three score and more people he's murdered, surrounding the house and peering in the windows at us, staring with their empty eye sockets, gore still caked to the cratered sides of their heads, and the mouth of each corpse set into a rictus like a dog baring its fangs. Some of them are propped against the wall, because Ezekiel also took their arms and legs to make them fit better inside the holes he dug for them. Those impatient spirits who still have hands left to them stand and scrape at the windows with their gritty fingernails. Most of them stand quietly, their flyblown forms blurring slightly against the flickering indoor light, pressing their ruined faces against the glass windows like little moons; their cadaverous expressions are expectant.

Another legion of cockroaches scampers across the floor boards, while a merry band of either squirrels or bats does the mambo in the attic.

"The worst kind of infestation!" Ezekiel is not frightened in the least by the walking dead or their more lively familiars among the animal kingdom. "Can't do anything with a pack of 'haints! Poison doesn't work, they don't even care if you set out traps that snap off their feet—they just keep shuffling about on their dusty old stumps! I've tried everything—I've put the torch to them, tried plowing them under with a backhoe and the strongest batch of lye I could cook up—I even doused them with holy water and they still keep coming around to bother me! Can't you hear their bellyaching?"

"No . . . "

"Well, I guess everybody sees an infestation differently."

"Are you sure they're dead? What if they're flesh-eating zombies, or something like that?"

'Zeke rolls his eyes to high heaven. "You think they'd be hanging around outside if they were? No, if they had that in mind, they're be in here gnawing on our guts right now. Besides, what're they going to chew with—look at the open maws on those grinning undead idiots—they've lost their teeth! They know good and well we aren't going to stand here while they try to gum their way through our leg bones. But they still pester me while I'm trying to sleep, and they won't stop their silly stunts like leaving their tongues in my stew kettle and leaking their ectoplasmic goo all over my bathtub. It's a nuisance, I tell you."

I still feel nervous, being surrounded by animated corpses and all. "Have you figured out how to clear them out?"

"I've tried everything. Like I said, poisons and traps are useless—I electrocuted them all just last week and they came back. Then I drilled them with a thousand buckshot shells two nights ago and made a bonfire out of their corpses, but they didn't even have the decency to stay gone one night. There's nothing harder to get rid of than an infestation of walking dead, take it from me."

"The only other thing I can think of is excavating yourself some tiger pits. If they fall in and get stuck on the stakes, then maybe you could pour some cement in on top of them."

"Done that, too—they just dig their way out like they do whenever I toss them back into their burial holes. Only one thing left to do now—give them what they want so they'll shut up and quit sloughing off their nasty decaying skin all over my windowsills and garden. Bunch of phantasmic nitwits."

Epilogue: Three years later, a rich developer bought Ezekiel's acreage at a land auction—since 'Zeke didn't have any kin to will it to and he'd only left enough to pay its taxes for a few years after he died. Oh, that developer was so happy; he bragged and bragged about how he was going to build a magnificent subdivision of new homes and a strip mall on that land. He stood to make a fabulous profit, and revitalize the town—or so he told everyone who would listen to him. People from all over the country would want to move to that beautiful piece of property—retirees, new families, people to work the new jobs he would create with his vision—and our town would be booming again.

The trouble was that the out-of-town developer didn't scout

Ezekiel's ground much beyond taking a helicopter flight over it before he bought the whole parcel at a ridiculous price; he'd wanted it for too long, even without setting foot, because he had heard so much about it. Everything looked good on paper—geological reports, property title, and so forth. When his surveyors went to map out that fine acreage, they came back with discouraging news:

The land was dotted with over sixty graves—nice, small granite markers with a name carved on each of them. They dug into one of the graves, found a corpse wrapped in a plastic tarp, and went running back to tell that developer the bad news. The city fathers declared the ground a cemetery and told the developer he couldn't put his subdivision and strip mall on the land, after all—they paid him a few cents on the dollar toward what he paid for the property (didn't even refund the money he'd paid out on permits and bribes), then announced plans to operate it as the city's new necropolis.

I did the carving of all those stones in secret so that nobody would associate them with me, then I would haul them in my truck out to Ezekiel's land late at night, and plant them over the graves after I pulled the cairns down. 'Zeke was able to give me most of their names before he died because he had hidden their personal items for self-preservation, or occasionally he'd had to talk with them a bit and ended up learning their names before busting their skulls; the ones he didn't have a name for were marked as "John Doe" or "Jane Doe", but that was better than nothing. It was the least I could for them—and for him. You see, THAT was what they had haunted Ezekiel for while he was dying; they hated the cairns he made for them and that they would remain as nameless in death as they were in life. Each of them wanted his or her own marker to show where they rested now. I'm lucky I had a big supply of granite on hand, and didn't have to order much more—that might have raised questions. But I needn't have worried: There was never any serious inquiry into the mystery of the graves on Exekiel's land. The local constables and city father are all too old to do much investigating. Besides, the old memorial park is too overcrowded to allow for the inevitable future of our town—a new boneyard is needed desperately to plant the rest of us aging citizens.

There's little to do anymore; I spend most of my time laying in bed by the window so I can watch my last days slowly pass by with each sunrise and sunset. But today I make myself dress and walk to the city's first graveyard to go see 'Zeke. He'd bought himself a plot there many years ago, since they refused to grant him permission to be buried on his own land like he wanted. The old cemetery is an overcrowded, haphazard jungle of stones, not a fraction as lovely as the new graveyard opening up on Ezekiel's acreage—the earlier town burial ground would have looked a lot better if I had carved all the tombstones instead of just some of them, and then set out every one of them by myself so they would look nice. I go to the place where Ezekiel is buried, and tell him the story of the poor developer; I know 'Zeke will love it, wherever he is now. I hope his spirit isn't in the dirt before me, lying under that rough rock cairn with his name pasted to a little metal stick at its foot.

You see, when I calculated out how much all those gravestones would cost—even small and plain as they were—Ezekiel decided to abandon work on his own marker to save money. He always was a cheapskate.

Grateful, the Dead

by Rich Handley

*Former newspaper reporter Rich Handley is the Managing Editor
of the trade magazine* Advanced Imaging, *and also serves as an
editorial assistant on Andromeda Press's* First Wave *comic book
spin-off. Rich has written for Lucasfilm's official magazines* Star
Wars Galaxy Collector, Star Wars Insider, *and* Star Wars Gamer,
as well as for the Star Wars *Role-Playing Game. A frequent writer
for* Star Trek Communicator *magazine, he has published articles
with* Cinefantastique, Toons, Sci-Fi Invasion, *and* Fandom.com.
*He is the author of several short stories and comics, including the
Dark Horse Comics tale,* Star Wars: Lady Luck, *which he co-wrote
with Darko Macan.*

    *Rich lives in New York with his wife, Jill, and their daughter,
Emily. Rumors that he is the next actor slated to play James Bond
are entirely unfounded, and largely the invention of his own limited intellect.*

    *Influences: The works of Neil Gaiman, Stephen King, Alan
Moore, Clive Barker, and Alfred Hitchcock. But more importantly,
real life, as a good chunk of "Grateful, the Dead" is autobio-
graphical—I'll let the readers wonder which parts!*

Grateful, the Dead

"It ain't much to look at and it ain't new," the old man with the pistachios said, flecks of red shell dotting his lower lip. "I'm tellin' you that up front so I don't get no complaints later. It's clean, it's freshly painted, and I ain't askin' much for it 'cause I usually rent to students. They ain't back 'til September, so the place is yours 'til then if you want it. But any repairs, you gotta handle, 'cause I go away to the Cape for the whole summer." He punctuated his words with a bloated finger permanently stained scarlet from years of pistachio consumption. He offered the bag of nuts to the young man behind him, but the latter politely declined.

Cole Whitland repositioned his knapsack so that it wouldn't hurt his shoulder. His light green eyes took in the wide living room area, the doorway to the kitchen and beyond into the poorly lit bathroom, another doorway leading into what looked to be a substantial bedroom, a curved stairway leading upwards, presumably to more bedrooms.

The old man was right about the appearance. The paint did little to hide the unsanded cakes of spackle lining the walls and molding, immortalizing countless tenants who had preceded him over the years. The rug was worn bare all over, particularly down the middle of the room, creating a cobblestone effect of sorts to the staircase. The faded curtains on the windows, the gas stove peeking out from the kitchen doorway, and the couch and chair that came with the apartment were forty years out of date and looked as haggard and tired as their unshaven owner. The slope in the floor was visible even to the naked eye, reminding Cole of the villains' lairs in just about every episode of *Batman* he'd ever watched as a kid. But, then, Cole didn't really care about the look of the place anyway. It wasn't aesthetic appeal that had drawn him here.

"I'll take it," Cole informed him quietly.

"Don'cha wanna look around first?" the Red Man asked, his drawl thickening even further. He lifted three crimson fingers to his mouth and deposited another batch of pistachios.

For reasons Cole couldn't quite define, the sight of the landlord's ruddy hand disturbed him, but he handed over eight $100 bills, just the same. Four hundred rent, four hundred security. "No, it's fine. I'll take it."

"All right," the old man shrugged, "suit yerself. But don't go callin' my place in Orleans two weeks from now, tellin' me the back yard's too small, the fridge ain't cold enough, and you want a reduction in yer rent 'cause the toilet wakes the dead when it flushes."

Cole raised an eyebrow at the irony of the man's words. Waking the dead was probably inevitable, regardless of what toilet he used. But he said only, "Okay."

The Red Man fished through the wide pockets of his ill-fitting overalls until he found a hefty set of keys. He handed them to Cole, along with a slight residue of pistachio shell and pocket lint, ticking them off one at a time. "Front door bottom lock, front door deadbolt, back door, garage door, thermostat box, basement inside, basement outside, and bat door."

That last caught Cole's attention, and he looked up in surprise. "Excuse me?"

"Bat door." The old man chuckled, a decidedly unpleasant sound that reminded Cole of his first car, a 1983 Ford Fairmont that refused to start on cold winter days. "One a'my former tenants used to call it that. Guess the name stuck. Here, I'll show ya'."

The landlord led Cole to the staircase, which curved out of sight to the left after three steps. Cole poked his head around the corner and gazed up the narrow, darkness-shrouded stairs. Half-way up, on the right-side wall, was a small metal door painted the same off-white as the wall, maybe three feet square. It was set into the wall a few feet above the middle steps and had a metal ring for a handle. Too wide to be a fuse box, too narrow for an entrance, it seemed wholly out of place in the middle of a wall. Cole caught his breath; he'd seen the door before, in the dreams, but hadn't recognized the name. What unnerved him more, though, were the eight nails holding the door in place, two on each side: thick carpenter nails, bent at 90-degree angles as though desperately trying to keep the door from opening. If the door had a key, he wondered, what purpose did the nails serve?

He watched as the Red Man turned each nail away from the door. It reminded him of old mummy serials he'd seen, where tomb-robbers pried open the dead, claw-like fingers of corpses to steal the treasured items with which they'd been entombed. "What's it for?" he asked.

"Nothin', really." The landlord took the key ring from Cole's hand and fumbled with it until producing a minute gold key, similar to those used on safety chests. This he placed in the lock and turned all the way around. With a metal "clank," the door opened. It hung crookedly, favoring the bottom hinge. "It's been here as long as I owned the place, goin' back a good twenty years or so, but I don't think no one's ever used it. It was prob'ly meant for storage when the house was built, but I got no idea what the hell they would'a kept in there. No light, no room to stand up, and it smells real bad. You'll prob'ly wanna just keep it locked, like everyone else did."

Cole craned his head, but with the lack of lighting in the stairwell, it was too dark to see more than a few inches inside the crawlspace. Unprepared for the dank pungency that assaulted him, he covered his mouth and nose with a sleeve. "Christ." He coughed and let the landlord close the door again without bothering to inspect it more thoroughly. "Why did your tenant call it the bat door? Should I be concerned about bats?"

"Nah, there ain't no bats in there. He just called it that on accounta he kept hearin' sounds comin' from inside. Said it sounded like bats flappin' 'round. Freaked him out. I dunno, I been here paintin' and repairin' for the past few days, and I ain't seen or heard a thing. Tell ya' the truth, I think he was doin' drugs. But in any case, that wasn't the reason he moved out so don't worry about it."

Cole wasn't worried. Or, more accurately, he was but it didn't matter. Now that he was here, he had to stay, bat door or no. He didn't fully understand why, but there wasn't any other choice. The house matched the one in his dreams so exactly, right down to the scratches on the painted metal door in the stairway, the so-called "bat door," that he knew it was all real. He had to see it through, no matter what. The dreams had been incessant, never letting up despite his efforts to ignore them; the images were too powerful, too horrible. It was only when he'd forced himself to confront them that his fear had abated and he'd begun to see them as instructions. In one particularly disturbing dream, he'd just been able to make out an address on a bloody envelope near a slot in the door: 13 Washington Street . . . the address he now called his own.

Cole set down his knapsack and let out a breath as he surveyed what would be his home for the immediate future. The Red Man continued talking. "Like I say, the students come back in September. That's their stuff in the bedrooms upstairs. I wouldn't mess with it if I were you; they're girls and you know how girls are about their things."

The landlord took one last look around, then walked to the front door, pausing as he opened it to add, "You got any problems you can't handle, you call Sastrowardoyo Realty. They know how to reach me when I ain't here. You and me'll get along great if they never call me. Best of luck to ya'."

He cackled and thrust another hungry handful into his gullet.

The next day, after settling in, Cole called his mother on his cell phone, not because he particularly wanted to talk to her, but because he knew her anger would increase the longer it took him to make the call. He hadn't told her where he was going when he'd dropped out of law school the week before, just that he was leaving and didn't know when he'd be home. His mother had been horrified, of course, just as he knew she would, but no amount of yelling, nagging, or pleading could dissuade him from his journey. It was just something he had to do, whatever the consequences (and he knew there would be many). For the sake of his sanity, he had to follow the dreams to their conclusion. Somehow, he knew that they'd never let up if he tried to ignore them.

One ring. Two rings. Three. Four. "Hello?"

"Hi, Mom," he replied in a low voice, steeling himself for the barrage.

"Cole? My God, Cole, how could you let me worry like that for a week? A whole damn week, Cole!" Cole winced. His devout Catholic mother blaspheming was never a good sign. "Do you know how scared I was? You drop out of law school, you call me and say you're going on some trip across the country—"

"Mom—"

"Don't you cut me off! I was worried sick! Your father would be furious about this, the Good Lord rest his eternal soul. Don't you care how your father would have felt? Don't you care how I feel? This is the most irresponsible thing you've ever done, and that's saying a lot, you know!"

"Mom, calm down. Please. There's no reason to yell, okay? Let's not turn this into a fight."

"So I should just be happy that you've taken your life and flushed it down the toilet? That you've thrown away everything your father worked so hard to give you? He put in all those extra hours on the force, Cole, never spending any of it on us, so you could go to law school and make something of yourself, and you thank him by abandoning our dreams for you eight months before graduation, and running off to God knows where!"

"Dad used to go away for weeks at a time, too," Cole replied, knowing the response to be a weak one, and that she'd call him on it. She did.

"Your father was a police detective," she replied, her scowl audible in her voice, "and when he went away, I always knew where he was going and when he'd be home! What's more, I always knew why he was going in the first place. It was his job! But you . . . you call and tell me you're dropping out of school, you don't give me any kind of explanation why, and then you wait a week before you bother calling back! I had no idea where you were, if you were in trouble, or why you were running in the first place! How could you do this to me, Cole?"

Cole exhaled slowly. "Mom, this isn't about you. It's not even about me, really. It's . . . well, honestly, I'm not really sure what it's about. But this is something I had to do. Please try to understand that."

"All I understand, Cole, is that your father would turn over in his grave right now if he knew what you were doing. He and I sacrificed so much for you so that you wouldn't ever have to, and you're throwing it all away! Dropping out of law school and running away like that . . ." Cole heard his mother's voice crack and he cringed. Although he could have predicted (and had, in fact) that his mother might cry when he finally called, it didn't make it any easier to hear, knowing it was entirely his fault.

"Mom . . ." he began softly, unsure how to proceed. In truth, he knew she was absolutely right. Leaving school to find a town and a house he knew nothing about, all because he'd seen them in a dream, had seemed insane to him as well. Hell, it still did. How could he argue the point with her, really? It *was* insane. "Look, I can't really talk right now. I have some things to do. But I didn't want you to worry about me."

"You're hanging up already? But you just called! We haven't had a chance to talk about what you're doing!"

"I'll tell you, Mom; I will. But now's not a good time. Just know that I'm doing all right, okay?"

He could hear the panic in her voice as she tried to comprehend. "But I don't even know how to reach you!"

"I'm in Oneonta, New York, but I'm calling from my cell phone. I don't know if I'll be staying long enough to have the phone in the apartment hooked up, but you can always reach me on the cell."

"You know darn well I can't reach you on your cell phone. I've been trying all week, and you never answer it."

"I wasn't ready to talk to anyone yet. I was afraid you might talk me out of it. I'm sorry. I will answer next time, I promise."

"You had me worried sick—"

"Mom," he cut her off, "I know. I'm sorry. I'll call you soon, okay? We'll talk. I have to go."

Her frustration was as audible as her words. "Just promise me that you're not in any trouble. I have to know the truth, Cole. Are you in any trouble?"

"No, Mom, I'm not in any trouble. I'll talk to you soon."

"All right," she said, but he knew it was anything but.

"Bye. Love you." He hung up before any more could be said.

Blood . . . so much blood . . . every wall awash in crimson hand-prints like some macabre mosaic . . . every window obscured by splatters of thick scarlet that ran in rich rivulets down the squalid panes and over the chipped wooden sills to pool on the carpet . . . how could so much blood spill from one body?

Cole screamed as the pearl-handled knife slashed downward once more, slicing open his left eye in a blindingly painful diagonal arc that severed the lower left section of his nose and split his lips and gums. The warm, syrupy river slopping from his bisected mouth told him that there was, indeed, still quite a bit more blood left to spill.

His heart threatening to burst from his chest, Cole sat upright on the couch so fast it made him dizzy. Exhausted from the long drive that had brought him here all the way from Wyoming, he'd fallen asleep on the musty sofa after a quick dinner of pepperoni pizza and Dr. Pepper. His eyes adjusted to the dim light and his breathing slowed as he analyzed the images in this latest dream. This time, it had been different. This time, he was no longer just an observer, but an active participant cast in the role of victim. Was he witnessing firsthand a crime that had occurred years before? Was that why he'd been drawn to this house, to receive its long-kept secrets?

Cole glanced up at a wall-clock, rubbing his eyes to remove the blur: 7:14, the clock told him, which obviously wasn't right. He'd have to fix that in the morning. He really needed sleep, but he waited a few more minutes to avoid finding himself in the same nightmare again. Finally, once his respiration and heart rate felt close to normal levels, he lowered himself back onto the cushion he'd been using as a pillow, and breathed deeply to relax his knotted muscles.

That was when he saw her.

Even in the low lighting, he could tell from her frail frame that she couldn't have been any older than twelve or fourteen. Standing with her profile facing him, her posture slumped as though in defeat, she had long ,thin hair that may have been either blonde or light-brown. It hung straight over her shoulders, obscuring most of her face, but what little he could see of her features seemed sad and delicate.

What struck him most, though, was the red robe she wore. It was quite long, spilling down from her neck well past her feet, and draped loosely over her shoulders, affording a rather ill fit. The sash of the robe hung low and appeared torn, while one arm hung limply at her side as though mimicking the sash.

She was entirely immobile and held a book in her other hand.

Cole was both alarmed and fascinated by the absurdity of finding a young girl standing in his living room in the middle of the night, silently perusing a book in lighting entirely inadequate to reading. He watched her silently for a moment, his skin tingling as he waited for her to move.

Finally, when it seemed she would neither change position nor acknowledge him, he hoarsely whispered, "Hello?" At her lack of response, he tried again: "Can you hear me?" After a pause, she began turning toward him, her face still obscured behind hair and book. Her legs didn't bend or shift at all during the turn, as if they'd been soldered to a slowly rotating platform built into the floor. The effect made him shiver, far more than he'd have expected from a girl so slight. He found it difficult to draw in breath.

For a few moments, neither moved or spoke. The girl's next actions, however, would be burned into Cole's memory for the rest of his days. With unexpected anger darkening her eyes, she lowered the book and raised her eyes to meet his. Without warning, her nose and upper lip clenched tightly in a cry of terror as her entire body left the floor to spring across the room toward him, impossibly covering the entire length of the room in a single furious leap. Her red robe billowed up around her like a great ruby sail as she closed in on him.

Cole screamed, but no sound issued forth from his throat, which had entirely constricted. He bounded up and backward against the couch back in a semi-standing position. He flung his arms in front of him as every muscle in his chest and shoulders tightened in stone cords. He clenched his eyes and steeled himself for the attack.

But it never came.

Opening his eyes, Cole again found himself alone in the room, though his heart was beating fast enough to accommodate two people. His eyes darted around frantically, and he dove off the couch for a nearby light switch, which he slapped several times before connecting.

"Shit!" he yelled, then yelled it again. "Shit!" He held one hand over his face, inhaling sharply. He tried to calm his breathing, but the effort offered little benefit with the vision still replaying in his mind. "Christ, holy shit!" Unable to remain inside, he bolted out to the front porch, slumped down onto the second step, and planted both hands firmly on his thighs. *This is crazy,* he told himself. *This is freakin' crazy. What in the name of hell was that?*

Cole buried his head in his arms for a moment, then swept his hair back and exhaled. The neighborhood was silent at this late hour, of course, but just the sight of the other houses helped him regain his composure. For a few minutes, he sat and considered what he'd just experienced, his perspective shifting as he did so. He was still terrified, but at the same time filled with an indefinable thrill at knowing it hadn't all been a dream, that he was, in fact, meant to come to this house. The girl's appearance cemented it.

"Sastrowardoyo Realty. Hartriono speaking." The voice on the other end of the phone was unfamiliar to him and had a slight Long Island accent, surprising in this neck of upstate New York. From the name, Cole guessed him to be Filipino.

"Hi, I was hoping you could help me. My name is Cole Whitland, and I need to know if there's been—"

"Mr. Whitland, yes, from 13 Washington Street, right?"

"Yes, it is," Cole replied, surprised that the man knew his name. "Have we met?"

"No, sir, I've not yet had the pleasure. However, Frank Toomi, the homeowner, phoned me yesterday to say you'd moved in. All settled in, then? Everything all right? Any problems with the house?"

"Everything's fine, thanks," said Cole. *Sure, aside from a dead girl in a red robe who nearly gave me a heart attack, everything's just great.* "Listen, I need to know if there's ever been any sort of trouble at that address." He knew how strange the question must have sounded, but he couldn't think of a better way to phrase it.

The realtor paused on the other end. "Trouble, sir? May I ask of what sort?"

"Well, to be honest, I'm not sure. Has anyone who lived there ever been hurt?"

"Hurt? As in an accident?"

"As in murder," Cole said, feeling faintly silly now at this line of questioning, which had seemed like a good idea while he was still dialing the number.

"Murder . . ." the man repeated. "Um, I don't believe so, Mr. Whitland. Mr. Toomi never mentioned anything unusual about the house. But, then, I only moved to Oneonta two years ago. May I ask why you would want to know?"

Cole considered how to answer, knowing the truth would sound absurd. "Oh, I'm just interested in the history of the house, that's all. It looks kind of old, and these old houses often have some great stories to tell. Who knows what ghosts could still be lurking about from ages past, you know?" Cole laughed half-heartedly, hoping he'd come off more convincingly to the realtor than he did to himself.

A slight chuckle conveyed the man's relief. "Oh, I see! Well, Mr. Whitland, even without looking it up, I think it's pretty safe to say that nothing out of the ordinary has happened in that house. Oneonta is a quiet town, and crimes so horrible are rarely ever committed here. Serenity and beauty, that's Oneonta's appeal. Murder . . . well, we leave *that* to the city-folk." The realtor laughed good-naturedly, apparently unaware how strongly his own "city-folk" accent gave him away.

Cole politely pressed the issue. "Well, just to be sure, can you look it up?"

"Unfortunately, I'm afraid we don't keep a database of that sort of information. However, if the subject really interests you, you might try the local library, on Saxon and Ford. The newspaper archives there go back a good hundred-and-fifty years or so."

"Thank you, I'll try that."

"You're welcome, Mr. Whitland, and if I come across any information on the history of that house, I'll be sure to contact you."

Thanking the man, Cole gave him his cell phone number and hung up, then grabbed his knapsack and headed for the Oneonta Public Library. The library, as in many rural towns, as in his own home town even, was cramped and smelled of must. The new and the old combined clashingly, with faded oversized and multi-volume tomes from decades past shelved not far from modern tables lined with computer terminals and rows of software CDs. A young child sat off to one side, unsupervised, pulling books from a shelf and stacking them haphazardly on the floor.

The reference librarian, a diminutive, balding young man who couldn't have stood any taller than five-foot-four, showed him where to find the past fifty years of *The Guardian*, Oneonta's local daily newspaper, on microfiche. Given the style of the girl's robe, Cole figured he probably wouldn't have to go back any further than that.

The first of several snags immediately presented itself, in that he had neither a name nor a date for his search, only an address. Unfortunately, though the *Guardian* was indexed by subject matter, he found no mention of 13 Washington Street anywhere, not even going back two decades further. There were reports of murders to be found, sure—probably more than the image-conscious agent at Sastrowardoyo Realty would have been comfortable admitting—but none at his particular address. Changing his tactic, Cole went on the assumption that the murder had never been solved. If that were the case, then the girl's abduction would have been reported but not in conjunction with that house, since the murder's location would not have been known.

Two hours later, his knapsack full to capacity with article printouts, Cole headed back to Washington Street. He'd researched dozens of unsolved murders committed in Oneonta in the past fifty years, involving girls between the ages of ten and eighteen (he'd widened the age range in case he'd gotten hers wrong in the midst of being so frightened). These, he planned to devour that night, not really sure what he was looking for but hopeful that they might yield a clue as to the identity of the girl in the red robe.

It was almost 1:00 in the morning by the time Cole had finished reading the last of the articles . . . for the third time. Determined to be as thorough as possible, he'd started over after his initial reading, then re-read them yet again for good measure. However, none of the photos resembled the girl from his vision, and after all his efforts, he was no closer to finding out who she was than he had been when she'd first appeared.

What the hell was he doing here? he asked himself, not for the first time that day. Despite the thrill of the search, the excitement of trying to piece together the clues that had brought him to this backwater town in the bowels of New York, the truth was that he felt entirely out of his league. A haunted house . . . a spirit chasing him around the living room . . . an aimless journey through some nowhere town inhabited by clichéd yokels like Frank Toomi . . . if he'd had a van, some chin hairs, and a dog with a speech impediment, he'd have fit right into an episode of *Scooby-Doo*. Cole pictured the Red Man shaking his fist as the sheriff pulled a little girl mask off his head. *And I would have gotten away with it, too, if it weren't for that meddling kid!* Exhausted, he chuckled hoarsely at the absurdity of it all. He needed to rest, clear his head, and start fresh.

But he found it difficult to sleep. He kept thinking about the girl in the red robe, how she'd completely and utterly terrified him while, at the same time, she made him want to know more. In truth, he knew so very little at this point. Even her having been murdered was an uncertainty, for all he had to go on was a dream.

But somehow, he was sure it had been a murder, and unsolved at that. Just as he was sure that he alone could help. He felt *connected* somehow to the events of her murder, though he had no idea how or why. Yeah, it sounded ridiculous, but the feeling lingered: it was up to him to put the girl's spirit to rest.

But how? So far, he'd turned up nothing. He thought about the phone conversation he'd had with his mother and wondered how his father would have judged his efforts: Detective Jason Whitland, a detective with the Wyoming State Police, decorated many times for his track record in solving the most unsolvable of cases. A dedicated career officer who'd hoped his son would follow in his footsteps, he'd been unable to hide his disappointment when Cole passed on a career in police work.

Still, his father had been proud of Cole's decision to go into law and soon got over his disappointment. "Cops and lawyers don't always see eye-to-eye, but we're on the same team," he'd once told Cole. "Never doubt that you're doing the right thing, Cole, and justice will attend to itself. That's all that matters."

Cole believed the truth of his father's words, even if he didn't entirely understand them. He pulled a picture out of his wallet, taken on Christmas many years ago. The image of his normally ultra-serious father, wearing the cream-furred bathrobe Cole had bought him and holding his five-year-old son up in the air, all bundled up in Christmas wrapping paper, was one he carried with him at all times. It was one of those precious times when Cole had felt truly close to his father. He held the photo up closer, grinning at the memory of his father wrapping him up in the discarded gift paper, and wished he were still alive so Cole could ask Detective Whitland for advice on what to do next.

He gazed sadly at the picture a few moments more, then returned it to his wallet and headed to his bedroom for some sleep. He paused in the doorway, looking back at the living room where the red-robed girl had appeared the night before, and wondered if she'd visit him again that night. Finally, he slapped the light switch and crawled into bed. As nervous as he was, he was asleep within seconds of hitting the pillow.

The noise that awoke him was horrendous: a piercing siren-like wail, backed by incredibly loud music, mostly drums with some poorly-played electric guitar and horribly off-key vocals thrown in the mix. Cole jumped out of bed and stumbled out into the dark living room. He groped for a switch, bathing the room in 75-watt brightness that stung until his pupils adjusted to the abrupt change in lighting. The cacophony blared on, indifferent to his need for sleep, and he realized it was coming from up-stairs, where the regular tenants' belongings were stored. It sounded like a radio, or an alarm. Both, actually. He squinted up at a clock to see what time it was.

7:14.

It took him a second to recognize the significance of the time: it was the same time the clock said when he'd awoken the night before. *Right before the girl in the robe appeared.* Adrenaline surged in his blood, removing any vestiges of sleep, as he read-ied himself for her return. He vowed not to let blind terror get in the way, as it had at their first encounter. This time, he'd main-tain control and reach out to her.

She didn't come, though. Standing alone in his living room a few minutes later, Cole felt disappointed and more than a little foolish. No vision. No girl. Just the nerve-wracking music blar-ing down at him from upstairs.

Hesitant to leave the room and miss her return, he eventu-ally crossed the living room and ascended the narrow staircase to the other bedrooms. He'd checked them out yesterday before going to the library and had found nothing out of the ordinary: dressers, un-linnened beds, assorted other pieces of furniture, and hordes of boxes in each of the three rooms, but nothing more. He'd tripped over a box in one room and hastily righted it, recalling Toomi's warning about girls and their things. Now, ap-prehension gripped him as ascended the stairwell once more, the music getting louder with each step. He passed the bat door and was relieved to discern that the sound was not coming from within.

At the top of the steps, Cole peered around the corner into each room. Nothing looked out of the ordinary, but now the music and siren-like blaring were so piercing he had to cover his ears. Whatever it was, the volume was far beyond the comfort level. In one room, he nearly tripped over something small: a portable alarm clock-radio, plugged into a socket in the wall and resting on its side on the floor. Cole realized he must have knocked it off a nightstand the day before when he'd toppled the girl's storage box. When that happened, it must have landed in just the right position to set the alarm.

Cole let out a small, guilty laugh at the rational, almost anticlimactic explanation for the music. Fumbling with the clock for a moment, he shut off both the alarm and the radio, then switched off the light and headed back downstairs. Before returning to his room, he detoured to the kitchen and poured a glass of Dr. Pepper. His mouth had gone dry, and the cold sweetness and soft fizzing would soothe him back to sleep on this blistering July evening. He tipped the glass back, draining it in one extended draught.

The music/alarm duet returned at its prior deafening level. Cole set the cup down hastily, almost missing the kitchen counter as he darted back into the living room and up the steps. Oddly enough, the clock-radio was still set to the "OFF" position.

Great, I broke the damn thing, he thought. *How do I turn this off if it's not "on" to begin with?* Annoyed, he unplugged the clock-radio and the wailing ceased once more. He set it back on the nightstand, stared uneasily at it for a moment, and turned to go back to his room. This time, he got halfway down the steps when the music started up again.

Cole stopped short on the steps. He'd turned it off. He knew he had. And he'd unplugged it. *How the hell was it still working?* He forced himself to turn and mount one step at a time until he could see into the bedroom.

There was the clock-radio, still sitting on the nightstand where he'd placed it. And there was the cord, dangling from its side, unplugged. He picked it up and turned it over in his hands. He opened the battery door and felt his mouth go dry once more.

There were no batteries inside the radio.

His hands shaking, Cole flipped the clock over again, desperate now to end the hideous discord pouring from it so he could think straight. As he turned it over, he saw that instead of the time, the digital display was rapidly flashing the number "1984."

Cole stared at the display, trying to comprehend what it meant, when the music and alarm stopped altogether. The abrupt silence was nearly as unsettling as the noise had been, even more so when it was interrupted by a young girl's whispered voice reminding him of his father's words, "Never doubt that you're doing the right thing, Cole, and justice will attend to itself. That's all that matters."

As though he'd been burned by flame, Cole jerked his hands away from the clock-radio, and it crashed silently to the floor. He turned without looking back and started down the staircase, stopping so quickly on the second step that he nearly lost his balance and plummeted headlong down the entire way.

The bat door was open.

That alone would certainly have scared him anyway, but what bothered him the most were the eight nails, each of which had been turned in the opposite direction by some unseen hand.

"Shit!" he yelled quite loudly, not really caring about the redundancy of his reactions to such situations. He had to get away from the upstairs bedrooms, but the only way down was past the bat door, and whatever had opened it was probably waiting for him inside that dark, dank crawlspace. Staring at it for several agonizing seconds, he balled up a fist and punched the wall to his right. Hard. "Ow! Shit!" The pain throbbing in his fingers made him wince, forcing him to focus on something other than sheer panic. He'd have to run past the door, for if he remained on the steps much longer, he feared he'd lose bladder control, or worse.

Okay, he thought, *no other way. One, two,* (he drew in a long breath) *three!*

Half-running, half-vaulting, he descended the stairs as fast as his feet would carry him, kicking the bat door as he passed. The metal door crashed back and forth with a reverberating "clang" and the taunting jingle of the handle-ring. Not stopping to shut it properly, he bounded out the door, off the porch, and into his parked car, where he sat catching his breath. After a few minutes, the oppressive silence unnerved him so he started the engine, cranked open the window, and turned on the radio.

The Grateful Dead broke the silence, reminding Cole "what a long, strange trip it's been." *You don't know the half of it, Jerry,* he told the radio. He flexed the fingers of his injured hand to make sure he hadn't broken anything. *I must be out of my damn mind. I'm no detective. That was Dad's game, and I'm obviously not him. Dad would never have run out of the house like that.* He rubbed his shin, which had impacted with the bat door a bit harder than he'd intended. *I should just put this car in Drive, head back the way I came, and keep going till I hit Jackson Hole. We don't have ghosts in Wyoming. We have jackalopes. We have Devil's Tower. We have Yellowstone and the Big Horn Moun- tains. But we don't have houses that try to scare the living crap out of people.* He looked over his shoulder at the house, now deathly still as though nothing abnormal had ever occurred. There was no way he was going back in until morning. *Why did you call me here? What in God's name do you want from me?*

Cole continued to stare at the empty house for a few more minutes, vainly trying to divine its purpose for him as he sorted through the clues he'd been given: a vision of murder, a visit from a soul in pain, the number 1984 (referring to the year, maybe?), the time 7:14, and a bat door that opened by itself.

And, he added, his father's advice, spoken in a young girl's whispered voice. He shook his head.

What did it all mean?

Images flickered past Cole as he skimmed through yet another roll of microfiche. He still wore the clothes he'd had on yesterday, and he was self-consciously aware that he needed a shower, but after waking up in the car, he hadn't yet been ready to go back into the house.

Still, the need to decipher the mystery gnawed at him, encouraging him to push past his fear. To that end, he'd returned to the library early that morning and had spent the better part of six hours poring over local newspapers from nearby towns, searching for any information on young girls murdered in 1984. This search yielded many more than the previous one, which was to be expected given the wider geographic area involved. He felt sickened at the number of young women whose lives had been snuffed out in violence in the course of just one year, in just this one part of the country.

Just when he was close to giving up for the day, Cole came to the July 24 edition of *The Star-and-Tackle*, a daily from the nearby town of Grange. He stared at the front page, stunned at what he saw there. Or, more accurately, who.

It was her.

The librarian printed out the article, which Cole voraciously devoured. Her name was Shawna Lippe, and she was twelve years old when she died. According to the article, a police officer had found her stuffed in a garbage bag on the side of a bridge. Or at least, he'd found *parts* of her in the bag. Several major organs had been missing, and her body had been sliced to shreds. The coroner determined that a hunting knife had been the murder weapon, and that the death had occurred on July 14.

Cole pulled out a pencil, jotted down "July 14," and considered the date a moment before crossing it out and rewriting it as "7/14."

He stared hard at the latter notation.

7/14.

He erased the back-slash and replaced it with a colon.

7:14.

In his mind, the numbers flashed wildly on the clock's digital display.

Cole found that his mouth had again gone dry, but he continued to read. When interviewed by a reporter, the officer who had found Shawna described a particularly gruesome wound: a deep knife-gash running diagonally across her entire face, from above her left eye down through her nose and lips, bisecting her face so badly it was hard to discern her bloodied features. The killer had sexually violated the young girl through the cuts in her chest, abdomen, and neck after she was already dead.

Cole winced. "Jesus, that's horrible," he muttered aloud.

No one had ever been arrested for the crime, Cole read, which was believed connected to eleven other unsolved murders in and around the Grange area. The murders occurred one year apart, between 1984 and 1995, each involving young women approximately the same age, description, and condition. The only difference was that whereas Shawna had been found in a bloodied robe and garbage bag, the others had all been wrapped in plastic. The police still believed the crimes connected, however, attributing the change to the killer refining his methods after his debut effort.

The killing spree inexplicably stopped in 1995. Shawna Lippe had been his first known victim.

Cole sat back to consider the implications. Twelve murders in eleven years, all unsolved and (he had to assume) occurring at Toomi's rental-house. Was he the killer? Is that why the image of his bloated, pistachio-stained fingers had bothered Cole so much upon their first meeting? Had he seen those same fingers, stained an entirely different shade of red, murdering Shawna Lippe in his dreams?

Scooping up both the printout and his knapsack, Cole rushed out of the library and started his car. He drove back to the Washington Street house, striving hard to avoid Oneonta's finest. All the while, he thought about the articles, the dreams, and his first meeting with the elder Frank Toomi. His heart raced. It couldn't be easy to satisfy the need to kill young girls in a small town, but Toomi had the perfect set-up to pull it off successfully—a rental home thirty miles outside the town in which he preyed, completely uninhabited a month or two each year when the students went home for vacation. Washington Street was filled primarily with student housing, which meant the chance of being witnessed with his victims was much lower than in other neighborhoods. Assuming he didn't know his victims, the Grange police would have nothing linking them to an old man from Oneonta. It all made so much sense. Hell, he was probably lucky he himself wasn't female, or his dreams might have gained some unwanted reality.

Oddly, Toomi apparently stopped his killing spree some time ago. Why, Cole wondered? Maybe he'd grown too old to feel secure in his abilities? Maybe he'd begun targeting other towns? Maybe (a morbid thought) the Red Man had gone impotent and could no longer fulfill the final act of his crime? Either was possible, but Cole would leave that to the police to determine. The Lippe girl's murder would no longer remain unsolved, and he knew he had the beginning of what was needed to lock the sick bastard away, unable to hurt any more children.

You were right, Dad, thought Cole with a tight smile. *You'd be proud of me. I was scared shitless, but I believed in what I was doing, and justice attended to itself. That was all that mattered.* Is that what it was like for his father on a case, he wondered? Cole pictured his father on Christmas, laughing hysterically while running around in his new bathrobe and holding up his gift-wrapped son. He grinned at the memory, his eyes glistening, and fervently wished his father were still alive so he could share this moment with him. The past five years had been very tough on Cole and his mother. So much had changed without Dad around. Even when his work would take him out of town on long-term assignments, they always knew he'd come back eventually. And he had, every time but the last, when some stoned-out psycho in Alabama made Detective Jason Whitland his final victim, moments before a barrage of police gunfire put an end to a long string of cop-killings.

By the time Cole pulled up in front of the house on Washington Street, his veins surged with adrenaline. He knew he might have a hard time explaining to the Grange police how he'd come to his conclusions—hell, he himself didn't really understand it—but he'd deal with any skepticism as he encountered it. Regardless of whether or not the cops believed in the supernatural, they'd have to take seriously the evidence against Frank Toomi, no matter how circumstantial. All it would take is one person to believe him and to look at the research—it was all there, literally in black-and-white.

Once back at the house, Cole threw his keys down next to his knapsack, adding his latest printouts to the previous batch. Downing a quick drink in the kitchen, he rushed back into the living room to retrieve the knapsack and keys. His hand stopped several inches from the bag, however, as his eyes locked with another pair from across the room.

For a moment, he said nothing, simply stared into the once-vital eyes of twelve-year-old Shawna Lippe. The terror she'd displayed at their first meeting was replaced by an air of sorrow. He felt no fear in turn, only grief at the pain she must have suffered, both in life and in death.

"Hello, Shawna," he tentatively began, his voice barely above a whisper. She said nothing in response. "We're gonna get this bastard, I promise."

He'd hoped that would elicit a positive response from her, but her expression remained unchanged. "No child should ever have to go through what you did," he added. "I have to admit you scared the hell out of me for a while there, but you did a good job of leading me where I needed to go. Thank you for letting me help you."

Still the girl stared quietly at him, the sadness in her face abating. Slowly she pivoted, as before, and began flowing fluidly toward the stairwell as though on unseen wheels. Unable to let go just yet, he called out, "Wait, don't leave! I need to know you're going to be okay!"

Without turning to face him, she paused for a few seconds at the bottom of the stairs before floating upward out of view. Curious, he followed. From the bottom step, he saw that she'd stopped before the unclosed bat door. With a single, pleading gaze at him, she abruptly rose off the step, hovered in mid-air for several seconds, and dissipated through the opening like sand flung into the path of a high-powered fan.

Cole drew in a sharp breath, startled at her unexpected exit. He viewed the aperture and slumped one shoulder against the wall. "You gotta be kidding me," he said, rubbing the bridge of his nose between thumb and forefinger. "Shit." Somehow, in his earlier self-congratulation, he'd entirely overlooked the opened bat door. He'd read enough Stephen King and Alan Moore as a kid to know better; ghosts rarely did anything arbitrary, and everything paranormal had meaning. He knew an invitation when it was handed to him, and this one didn't thrill him in the least. *Here, Cole, climb into this stinky hole, will ya'? The spirits need you to do some light dusting and hang an air freshener for them before you go. There, that's a good boy.*

Cole shook his head in resignation. *I've come this far,* he thought. He grabbed the knapsack, fished out a pocket flashlight he carried everywhere, grabbed a clean sock as an afterthought, and began a measured ascent to the middle of the steps. He thought about finding a weapon of some sort, but what good would it have done him, really? He shined the flashlight into the crawlspace, holding the sock up to his nose to filter out the stench. The space went back a good twenty feet or so, sloping down on either side in accordance with the pitch of the roof. He considered the geometry of the house and realized that whoever had built the place (or maybe Toomi himself) had closed off the garage ceiling and removed the center beams, creating a storage area that was quite deep but no more than a few feet high. From the rotting essence wafting through his sock, he was beginning to suspect what had been stored within.

Cole moved the light around, outlining the criss-crossed rafters and creating an illuminated column of disturbed dust. Not the kind of place he wanted to explore, even under the best of circumstances, as he was very claustrophobic. "Shawna?" he called, in the vain hope of finding out what she needed without his having to go in there. Not unexpectedly, he got no response save for the echo of his own words as they bounced around the lengthy enclosure.

Breathing deeply to calm the anxiety that always accompanied tight spaces, Cole set the flashlight inside the crawlspace and faced the opposite wall. He reached back with both hands, tightly grasping the sides of the opening, and pulled himself into the hole. He crossed his legs in a seated position, mindful of the sloping rafters running parallel to the roof not far overhead, and sat motionless for several seconds before proceeding. Finally, he shimmied his way deeper into the tight compartment, darting the light around like a half-asleep laser-show operator.

"Okay, I'm here," he announced, as much to be comforted by the sound of his own voice as to connect with the forces that had somehow coerced him to do this. He breathed in and out, in and out, consciously reminding himself not to notice how cramped the space was, but all the more conscious of it for the effort. "I'm in. I came in. I'm here. Now what?" As expected, he got no response. He continued his breathing routine, all the while scanning the space for some sign of what the girl had wanted him to find. "Look, I'm not following you on this one. I'm trying, but I just don't see anything." Still no response. He flashed the light right and left, craned his neck to scan the rafters, and took one more pass around all four walls before throwing his hands up in the air. He was suddenly acutely aware just how narrow the space was, and he felt dizzy. His breathing quickened, his heart pounded through his shirt, and his limbs were getting weak.

That's it, he decided, recognizing the onset of hyperventilation. *I'm getting out of here. Now.*

He repositioned himself to scurry back to the opening but only advanced a few feet before the metal door slammed shut. To his horror, he recognized the scraping of metal on metal as the same unseen hand that had turned the eight nails open now completed the circle by turning them closed again, one by one.

Cole's gaze shot frantically around the wooden tomb, his irrational mind sensing the aged floor boards and rusty-nailed two-by-fours closing in from all sides. "Oh Christ, Oh God, no please no, Christ, no no no!" His breath now coming in jagged gasps, he rocked back and forth in panic-stricken denial then jerked around onto his back, desperate to get his legs out in front of him and kick the door open. Scampering toward the door like an overturned beetle, he slammed both feet repeatedly into the door, which didn't budge, not even slightly. It was as if something were firmly pushing on it from the other side, something immensely strong.

"Why?" he yelled. "Why are you doing this to me? I don't understand! How am I supposed to put an end to all of this if I'm stuck in here? Come on, let me out, please!" The empty response sent him into a frenzied attack as he kicked and screamed and swung blindly with both hands. As he did so, a sudden sharp pain cut through his right hand. His fist had impacted on the back end of a broken nail and was now bleeding quite profusely. The pain was searing, stinging his eyes with salted tears and snapping him out of his panic long enough to draw his attention away from the door and to the nail. Stuck to it, stained dark brown, was a scrap of cloth.

Cradling his bleeding right hand in his left armpit, grunting at the effort of moving around within the crawlspace, he reached forward with his undamaged hand and held up the flashlight so he could examine it. He dislodged the cloth from the nail. The scrap seemed to be terrycloth, its original color long since rendered undetectable by time, by whatever brownish fluid had stained it, and by his own blood now adorning it. Despite the color discrepancy, he knew instinctively what it was: a piece of the girl's robe.

Is that why she'd led him in here, then prevented him from leaving? To make sure he found the cloth as a final piece of evidence so that his story about Toomi would be treated seriously? He wondered if she were watching him now.

Without fanfare, the door opened, bathing him in sorely appreciated light. Just when he'd thought she was trying to kill him, it appeared she'd again been helping him. Unwilling to risk having the door close again, he half-crawled, half-vaulted for the door, then tumbled out onto the staircase, where he lay gasping for several minutes, thankful to be out of the hole. When his breathing was close to normal again, he stood and reached up to close the bat door, when he noticed something he hadn't seen before. One of the boards in the floor, just inside to the right of the opening, had apparently been cracked during his attempt to kick the door open. It now jutted out of a small hole in the floor. Retrieving the flashlight, which was just within arm's reach of the door (otherwise, he simply would have left it in there), he pulled the broken board out and shined the light into the hole created by its removal. To his surprise, the light went down a couple of feet, an unusually deep distance between the crawlspace floor and the garage ceiling. *What an inefficient use of space*, he mused. *Why the heck would they have done that?*

Shining the light around the floor, he noticed the barely concealed outline of a doorway, which would not likely have been visible to anyone not actively looking for something out of the ordinary. He wrapped a dust-tainted sock around his gouged hand and grabbed the floor on both sides of the hole, ignoring the pain as he lifted out a large section and slid it noisily onto the solid floor beyond. The volume of dust suddenly sent airborne made him cough as he bent over to shine the flashlight into the hole. The scene inside made him gag and nearly vomit.

Like some horror movie caricature of a high school biology lab, the hidden storage area was filled with glass jars, each containing what looked to him to be human remains. Slightly decomposed from the limited air trapped inside when the jars had been sealed, the remains still retained recognizable forms. The stench was overpowering now, a sign that the seals were not completely air-tight. *The missing organs*, he realized, feeling the bile rise in his throat. *I don't even want to know what the goddamn psycho needed those for.* Something reflected the light back at him, and he discovered that three of the jars had been broken open, their contents long since deteriorated.

More likely eaten, he amended, nauseated at the thought. Rats, or some other vermin, must have gotten into the crawlspace, attracted by the odor. That must have been what the former tenant had mistaken for bats, Cole realized. Had the man known that the "flapping" sound freaking him out was actually the sound of furred creatures feasting on human flesh, would he have been comforted? Cole severely doubted that.

Leaving the bat door open, Cole collected his wits on the couch before alerting the police. What with the library articles, the swatch of blood-stained cloth, and the biological evidence under the floor boards, there was little doubt Frank Toomi would be put away. The police would take one look in the crawlspace, Cole was sure, and issue an immediate order to extradite the aged murderer from Massachusetts to face trial. They'd be able to close the books on at least the twelve cases he knew of, and who knew how many others. Given his age, he'd probably die in prison.

The words of Jerry Garcia came back to him, and he nodded soberly. *What a long strange trip, indeed, Jerry.*

Before heading out, Cole thought he should call his mother and let her know not to worry, that it was all over. She picked up the phone on her end immediately, as though she'd been waiting for it to ring.

"Cole?" The urgency in her voice made him feel extremely guilty, but he hoped she'd understand once he explained it all to her."

"Hi, Mom. It's me."

Her words poured out like water from a spigot. "Oh, thank God. I've been so worried about you. This is killing me." He heard a sniffle from the other end, but said nothing, knowing after all these years that although she might have paused, she wasn't done talking. "I don't know what you're doing, and I haven't been able to think about anything else."

"I know. I'm sorry," he said simply.

"I want to be supportive, Cole. I do. I'm your mother. I want to tell you you're an adult and that you're free to make your own decisions because you're the only one who has to live with them. I know that as the mother of a 24-year-old law student, I'm supposed to say all that. But this is just so crazy. You haven't even told me why you left."

"It's okay, Mom. Everything's okay now."

"I want to believe that, Cole, but this is all so unlike you."

"You're right. But the definition of what is or isn't unlike me is changing."

"I don't understand what that means. I don't know how to answer that, even."

"You will. Honest. For now, just know that I'm fine. Trust me, okay?"

There was a long pause on her end. "You're sure you're not in trouble? Please tell me if you are, Cole, and I'll help you. But you have to tell me, so that—"

"I'm not in trouble," he said, cutting her off gently. Her pleas to let her help him reminded him of his own plea to Shawna Lippe's spirit, and he didn't want to upset his mother any more than he already had. "I did what I came here to do, and I'll be coming home once I've tied up a few more things here. Then I'll explain it all, okay?"

His mother sighed, exasperated. "All right, Cole." She changed the subject. "How's Oneonta this time of year?"

"Hot," he laughed.

"Your father used to visit that area every year, you know."

That took Cole by surprise. "He did?"

"For that annual criminology conference he liked to attend in Otego. You know the one. He always drove us crazy spouting forensics jargon for weeks afterward."

"Oh right, that," he replied, suddenly uneasy but unable to say why. "I'd forgotten where they held that."

"Otego's only a few minutes east of Oneonta. Jason liked to stay in Oneonta because he found Otego pretty boring, and in July, there's always more to do in a college town than in a backwater hole like Otego."

Cole frowned. "What was that, Mom?"

"I said there's always more to do in a college town," she repeated.

"No, before that. You said he went to Oneonta in July?"

"Every year for twelve years. Right up until the year he passed on, God rest his loving soul. Why?"

Every July for twelve years. Cole's throat went dry.

"July 14?"

"What? I don't know. The date changed every year. It was always on a weekend. Cole, you sound upset. What's wrong?"

Cole loudly cleared his throat, which hurt like hell, and tried to recall the details of his father's trips to New York. When he'd been younger, he didn't care enough to ask for details, and by the time he was old enough, he'd already gone away to school. "Uh . . . did Dad stay at a hotel when he came into town?"

"No, he had an arrangement with a retired policeman from

that area. Your father knew him from the conference, and he was nice enough to let your father stay at an apartment he rented out since it was during the college's summer vacation and he didn't have any renters." His mother's words made Cole ill, and he tried to stifle a shiver. "He didn't charge anything since they were fellow officers, so Jason brought him a couple of pounds of Moose Mountain pistachios each year as a thank you."

Cole wanted to yell. Or cry. Or hang up. Or do anything but listen to any more of this. But he had to know. For God's sake, he had to know. His voice barely a croak, he asked, "Do you remember the man's name?"

"Cole, my God, what's wrong? You said everything was okay— why are you asking me these questions about your father?"

"Mom, I have to know," he barked, more harshly than he should have. "What was the man's name?"

"I . . . I don't remember. What's this ab—"

"Was it Toomi?"

His mother's voice was badly shaken now. "What?"

"Mom, this is very important. Was the man's name Frank Toomi?"

"Yes, I think it was. Cole, talk to me, what's going on? You're scaring me!"

Cole let the phone down fall from his hand and crossed his arms over one another protectively. This couldn't be. It had to be a coincidence. That's right, the biggest cosmic fucking coincidence in the history of mankind. He couldn't accept the alternative, so a coincidence it was.

He felt a hand on his shoulder and looked up to find Shawna Lippe gazing wordlessly at him. He was startled, as he hadn't heard or seen her approach, but not afraid. Her face exuded sympathy and sorrow, not for herself this time, but for him. Tears poured from his eyes as he saw in her face the confirmation of his fears.

She held out a hand to him. In it, she held the cloth swatch. He took it from her, saw its tattered sides, felt what little remained of its terrycloth texture. He identified the brownish stain he'd noticed earlier: it was blood. Presumably hers. As he did so, she changed. More accurately, the robe did. No longer uniformly red, it took on a sickening pattern of droplets and splatters, the background adopting a light cream color.

Cole looked back and forth from Shawna to the cloth scrap in his hands, then back up to the girl again. The sash was ripped, as though one end had been torn off in a rush. Or caught on a nail.

He closed his eyes . . .

. . . *and when he opened them again, the scene around him had altered. The house was still the same, but some of the furniture was different. The rug didn't look as old, and there was a television in the living room that hadn't been there a moment ago. Strange, he noted, bewildered. Everything looks taller. No that wasn't quite right. Nothing else was taller. He was just seeing it from a different height. He'd gotten shorter.*

I'm her, he realized with amazement. It's 1984, and I'm seeing what Shawna did. I'm seeing her murder, firsthand. And not just as a dream image, he realized. This had a feeling of reality to it. Again, he felt a hand on his shoulder, but when he looked up, it wasn't the hand of a dead girl that rested on his shoulder.

It was the hand of his father. And the eyes glaring down at him burned with an intense anger he'd never before seen in his father's face. It terrified him far more than anything he'd experienced in the past several days.

He tried to pull away, but his body was that of a twelve-year-old girl, and his father was too powerful. He saw the glint of steel, felt the first slash as it swung down hard into his arm, rending flesh and muscle from bone. He screeched in agony as blood sprayed across his father's enraged face. A second cut, a third, a fourth. And more. Many more. He heard himself screaming, felt time slowing, and knew that consciousness would soon ebb away.

Blood . . . so much blood . . . every wall awash in crimson handprints like some macabre mosaic . . . every window obscured by splatters of thick scarlet that ran in rich rivulets down the squalid panes and over the chipped wooden sills to pool on the carpet . . . how could so much blood spill from one body?

Cole screamed as the pearl-handled knife slashed downward once more, slicing open his left eye in a blindingly painful diagonal arc that severed the lower left section of his nose and split his lips and gums. The warm, syrupy river slopping from his bisected mouth told him that there was, indeed, still quite a bit more blood left to spill.

He'd been through this all before, but the pain was so much worse this time, for the knowledge of his killer's identity hurt far worse than any blade ever could.

Cole's eyes shot open. He was back on the couch, and Shawna was standing sadly before him. With trembling hands, he embraced her to him and sobbed. "I'm sorry," he said between tears. "I had no idea what he was."

"I know," she said, pulling away gently. It was the first time, he realized, that she'd spoken to him directly.

"He wrapped you up in his robe, didn't he? The one I got him for Christmas a few years before that. He hadn't planned for so much blood. It's why he changed to plastic after the first murder, so there'd be less to clean up, and less chance of getting caught."

She nodded.

"My father always tried to teach me about justice," he stammered weakly. "How could he do something like this?" He wiped the tears from his eyes, his face numb.

She rose gently off the ground as she responded, "Never doubt that you're doing the right thing, Cole, and justice will attend to itself." Pained at the use of his father's words, he watched her rise toward the ceiling. Turning to whisper "Thank you," she dissipated entirely, and he knew he would never see her again.

For a while, he sat expressionless on the couch, shattered by the knowledge of what his father had been, and how close he'd come to having an innocent man sent to prison. He knew it would be a very long time before he'd ever be okay again. But he knew what he had to do. His father had taught him well. As he reached for the cell phone to notify the police, he hoped his mother would some day forgive him.

A New Ripper

by John Barrow

There's nothing you need to know about me that has anything at all to do with reading this story. Stories aren't about writers. They're about stories.

A New Ripper

The night . . .
The night is not a time; it is a *place*, you see. A state.
More accurately, a state of mind.
They say God made man in his image.
You know what that means, don't you?
It means that God is insane.

Night is for . . . the *special* people. The ones who are too mighty, too loud, too *different*. They skitter forth when the sun's rays have died, like vampires who fear Apollo's gaze.

Some of them are drug addicts, searching the city streets for their next score, the next big hit. Some are pimps, making sure that business is going as usual. Still more are simply worshipers of the night, exulting in its sultriness and its unbridled sensuality.

See, you can get away with things at night, things that in the light of day are impossible or unthinkable. Because the night covers everything with its all-encompassing darkness.

People may think that electricity fights off the night, but they're wrong. The night is magic, and it shields those who are good to it.

So now we have set the scene: You see broken-windowed buildings downtown, each one a jagged, gap-toothed mouth. Whores, crackheads, and random wanderers trolling the streets.

Now put it in the future. Some indefinable time from now. Instead of neon, holographic signs blink and jitter. Patrol bots jerk along the sidewalks, occasionally rousting innocent tourists because they happen to have put on the wrong color cap, a color that triggers the bots' gang database subset. Just far enough in the future that you can still recognize the players.

Are you paying attention?

A jet-black turn of the millennium sports car pulled up to the street corner with a sound like a hiss. The passenger-side window buzzed down and the driver gestured to the four working girls on the corner. They looked at each other quickly. Ginny, she had just come back from a "date." Starr was still gettin' flashes from that bad bloodrock, and Violet kept complaining about her back. Not a word passed between the four. Jane (as in "Jane Doe" she told the johns) agreed to go.

She leaned into the car. Her flaming red hair cascaded over her shoulders, spilled down into her cleavage, which was squeezed by something golden and tight and low-cut. Leaning over hiked her miniskirt up even farther than usual, and anyone walking behind her could tell that she didn't believe in underwear.

The driver . . . a tall guy, a little over six feet maybe. Respectable-looking enough—business suit, tie, the whole deal. Just another stiff from the suburbs whose wife wouldn't do some of the nastier stuff.

"What's up, baby?" she cooed.

"What's your name?" he asked.

"Jane." She flashed him her quick, seductive smile. She convinced herself it was seductive, anyway, after being told she was beautiful by a john who fell ridiculously in love with her and then OD'd on 'rock.

"Of course." He hit a stud on his door and the passenger door unlocked. "Get in."

Not a chance. Did he think she was some dipshit low-Q cunt from upstream? "We gotta talk money first—"

"Money's no problem." He pulled a hundred-cred out of his pocket and flipped it at her. "Two more when you're done."

She examined the cred. It looked real. She slid it against the scanner in her left bracelet just to make sure.

Gold mine! Three hundred bucks for one goddamn trick! The local Prostitute's Guild only took 75 a trick, so she'd get away with more than 200 for herself . . .

She practically leapt into the seat, slamming the door. The driver hit the gas. As the car squealed away, Jane blew a kiss to the girls on the corner.

She started to give him directions to her usual hotel. A ten-cred for the room and another for the watchman to page the room if a 'banger crew decides to invade. But before she could say anything, he took two lefts and a right—headed straight for the hotel.

"Will this facility suffice?" he asked as he pulled into the parking slot.

"Yeah . . ." She rubbed her palms, sweaty against her skirt. "I usually come here." The double meaning hit her as soon as she said it, and she laughed, throwing back her head to give him a good look at what he was buying. Say what you want about Jane Doe—she earns her creds.

"Of course," he said, exactly the way he'd said it before.

They went in through the back door, which surprised her. She was about to ask him about that when he beeped open a nearby door and took her into the room.

He flipped on the lights and kicked off his shoes. He headed straight for the bed and lay down on it.

Once inside and in such a familiar setting, Jane lost all of her questions in the far corners of her mind. She was too busy calculating that extra two hundred.

This guy'll want the mouth-work, she predicted. *All the way. He's got that tight look.*

As she began to peel off her clothes, the man grunted a "No." She looked at him quizzically. "That won't be necessary," he informed her. "Come here."

He pulled down his fly, then reached inside and pulled out his erection. By Jane's standards, it was nothing to write home about. Average size, just another cock. Its one outstanding feature was the lack of pubic hair. Jane appreciated that. One thing she couldn't stand was the mouthful of hair that inevitably resulted from serious deep-throat action.

With the ease of an experienced master, Jane kicked off her shoes and positioned herself on her stomach on the bed, her face just above the man's groin. She kissed it gently, then followed up with a tentative lick.

"Just suck me," he growled.

What a hard case! Still, he was bankrolling all this shit . . .

She took him into her mouth. Years of practice took over as she bobbed her head up and down, sucking in at the same time. She teased her tongue along his underside the whole time, managing to go from root to tip while still keeping him in her mouth. She was careful to keep her lips pulled over her teeth.

Up and down. Up and down. His slick cock throbbed in her mouth, brushed against the back of her throat. His steadily increasing moans told her to keep up the tempo. She shifted her tongue, concentrating on stroking the rich bundle of nerves just beneath the head. His hands found her head, gripped her, forced her into a faster rhythm. His fingers, entwined in her hair, were incredibly strong, pressing firmly against her skull. He forced her to go faster, his hips rising to meet her face with each manic thrust. Then both hands slipped lower, cradling her face, holding her mouth tightly around him. Her jaws began to ache and she hoped he'd come soon.

He bucked suddenly, almost screamed, and forced her down all the way on him, so that her nose was pressed against his pelvis. She felt his penis against the back of her throat and readied herself for the machine-gun rapidity of a man's ejaculation.

His first shot of ejaculate was tremendous. It made a noticeable impact in her throat, such that she instinctively tried to pull away. He held her fast and she swallowed with some difficulty.

The second load, impossibly, was even larger. It filled her mouth and ran thickly down her gullet. She swallowed again.

The third was at least a pint. It went right down her throat. She started to gag, but he still held her on him, moaning in pleasure, writhing.

Now he was coming even more. No longer was his climax a series of spurts—no, he was experiencing one long, continuous ejaculation, forcing a huge quantity of semen down her throat at an incredible velocity. She was choking on it, there was so much. She beat at his legs with her hands, but he still held her fast. His seed rocketed down her and into her. In foggy desperation, she bit down on his member, expecting a shriek (she'd done it before), but instead he just kept going.

Redness began to creep around the edge of her vision as she tried, unsuccessfully, to continue swallowing. She raked his thighs with her fingernails, but nothing happened. One nail broke off and when she tried to scream, she wound up with sperm in her airway, heading for her lungs.

Now her stomach was filled with him. She could *feel* it, could feel the slimy heaviness in her belly. Still more pumped into her. Her esophagus began filling up and she tried, desperately, to vomit.

She couldn't breathe. She tried to take a breath, but his spend only blocked her up.

She began thrashing on the bed, as if she, too, were experiencing an incredible orgasm.

She twitched. Moaned.

The man stopped writhing in pleasure. He held the woman in place for thirty seconds, then released her face. Her mouth slid away from his cock as her head dropped to one side. Her eyes were unblinking and vacant. Semen and saliva flowed from her mouth, and some of his seed was draining through her nostrils. Along his cock were teeth marks where she'd bitten him in an effort to stop him.

There was a movement under the bed, and a small, ugly man rolled out into the open. He was naked.

He climbed up into the bed, ignoring the driver. The ugly man's eyes danced excitedly. He positioned himself behind Jane and pulled up her miniskirt. He gaped at her buttocks and grabbed his crotch, stimulating himself into an erection all of three inches long. The small man separated Jane's buttocks and inserted himself. "Ohhhhhhh!" he shrieked, face alight with joy. "Mommy! Mommy!" He started pumping in and out enthusiastically.

The driver dispassionately cleaned off his cock with Jane's hair, then tucked himself back into his pants.

"Mommy so good so good ohhhhhhhh!" chanted the small man.

The driver sat up on the bed and stared blankly ahead, apparently not noticing anything at all.

"mommymommysogoodiloveitohthisasslikeyousohmommy andbrotherfuckyouallmommymommmymommy!!!!"

The small man came in just a few seconds. He withdrew his rapidly softening member from the dead woman and caught his breath. Then he pulled the lone suitcase from the closet. In it were two sets of clothing for himself, another set for the driver, and several jars.

He took one of he jars and walked over to the driver. The driver obediently opened his shirt. The small man opened a panel on the driver's chest and upended the jaw, pouring into the hole a whitish, sticky fluid.

"All drained, hmm?" the ugly man asked. "Drained!" He giggled. "Mommy! Not drained any more, oh no!" He shook the last few drops in and then closed the driver.

The small, ugly man dressed and the driver took the suitcase. They turned off all the lights, and, after locking the door, went to the car and drove away.

The night, smiling with starlight, guarded their escape.

Because the night enjoys this sort of thing. Really.

God made man in his image. Ergo, God is insane.

And what else, really, do you expect an insane creature to do, if not to create creatures even worse?

Sleep tight.

Common Cold

by Liam C. Grey

Liam C. Grey claims residence in Baltimore, MD, and New Brunswick, NJ, depending on what type of project he is working on. Well rounded in the arts, Mr. Grey has appeared in the touring company of Les Miserables, *spent time on stage in a Johnny Cash cover band, and is currently hard at work producing his first film. "Common Cold" represents his first return to prose writing in four years, as well as his first published work.*

Mr. Grey prefers dogs to most humans and lives with his Siberian Husky, Sabrina.

Common Cold

The old cashier barely has time to give you a quick glance before jerking her head to the side.

Eh—cah–kahf!

You offer her a Kleenex, which she accepts. She wipes her mouth tenderly and, hand shaking, drops the tissue into a basket.

"Thank you. Will that be all?"

You smile. Your motley collection of a tube of Tums, a four-pack of toilet paper, two bottles of soda, and a lonesome Snickers bar can't be anyone's idea of a weekly shopping trip, but this will have to do for a day.

"I think so. But if I catch your cold, I might need to add some NyQuil."

Mrs. Diamond returns your smile. She passes the toilet paper beneath the electronic scanner. BEEP!

"I can't remember the last time I was sick. I think my grandson gave it to me."

"Ah. The good and the bad of his visit."

"And his new girlfriend was the ugly."

BEEP!

"Ouch."

She coughs again. "I wish they would find a cure for the cold. Been dealin' with it for seventy years. Isn't that long enough?"

BEEP! BEEP!

"Maybe they will."

She coughs again, this time covering her mouth with her palm.

"Not in my lifetime."

BEEP!

"Seven nineteen. I mean, $7.20, please."

You hand over one of the new five dollar coins from your cash clasp and reach into your pocket for the loose change.

"Maybe not." You hand her two dollar coins and a quarter.

"I'm sorry?"

"Maybe they won't find a cure. But, then again, maybe they will." You pick up your bag and flash her another smile before heading to the door. In the reflection on the display glass, you catch a glimpse of the old woman shaking her head as she drops a nickel into a tray on the counter.

"Have a good night!" she calls.

"You too, Mrs. Diamond."

The engine of your Firebird roars as you force the speedometer to 50 on the sidestreets toward home. The night breathes black and alive outside of the car, cut only by the twin swords of light from your halogens and the mindless droning of the news on the radio.

". . . Nasdaq down eighty-two points . . . the Bullrushers tie a club record with nine turnovers in their loss today . . . mayor says the investigation will continue . . . no word yet on the missing schoolbus full of children that disappeared . . ."

Missing. That word echoes in your head. Your lunch buddy at work, Frank, has been out all week. You haven't really thought of it much until now, probably just a vacation he told you about and you forgot. Typical. The guy goes on vacations more than he works, or at least, it seems that way. But, supposedly he's worth it. Can't blame a company for giving a guy what he deserves. Wish they were all like that.

A story breaks through your zombied driving state and beckons your hand to the volume control on your steering wheel.

"Another fatal accident on our city's freeways today. A late model Ford Expansive struck a pedestrian who was apparently stumbling between the number two and number three lanes going eastbound on the Crosstown Freeway. Based on the condition of the victim's body, police estimate the Ford's driver was traveling between . . ."

You decrease the volume. That makes, what . . . five, six, seven pedestrians killed on freeways in the past month? What are these people thinking? Freeways are for driving, not walking.

Your speedometer slips to 45.

A lonely, moderately warm TV dinner looks back at you from your kitchen table. Steam rises up from the mashed potatoes, but you already know from past experience that the Salisbury Steak will be an ice cube in the middle. Better than nothing, though. The silence of your empty apartment is disturbing, to say the least. But, you're used to it. Since the day you started working at DyNAmic Labs, this nothingness has taken over and embraced you instead of rejecting you. It is your sound, the sound of a life dedicated to a thankless job that has never produced any positive results, and probably never will, at least, not in your lifetime.

Not in my lifetime.

You stop thinking of that. You wonder if Frank will be back tomorrow.

Now, where's that fork?

The Firebird's door opens silently. The keys barely jingle as you turn the ignition and the engine sparks alive. Vented air, somehow brisk and burning at the same time, blows into your face as you turn onto the road that leads you to work.

Again, you feel the zombie taking over. The radio bellows

out its nonsense. Other cars pass by in a flurry of motion, going past you and behind you, but the nothingness from your apartment has spread to the dome of your automobile. As an automatic pilot, you mindlessly turn right, then left, then left again, already knowing to slow down for the stoplight ahead. The zombie is in control. Yet even the zombie cannot sleep through everything.

Helicopter blades drone through the voice from the radio:

"Jim, I'm looking right now at the Lakeside Highway, where there are still multiple backups for miles. It looks like . . . yes, the police are still on location here, trying to remove the last of the children from the highway. As AM 1010 first reported to our listeners, about an hour ago traffic came to a dead stop due to several dozen children playing in the middle of the road, unwilling or unable to move! Police have been on the scene for about forty-five minutes, but with rush hour only fifteen minutes old, it's going to be backed up here for a long time to come. I'm Kris Lightner, back to . . ."

You slam on your brakes, praying that there's no one behind you. The stench of burning rubber presses in from the vents, filling your lungs. The Firebird lurches to a halt–the rearview mirror reveals no danger from behind.

"–hope you listeners aren't planning on taking the Lakeside–"

You mute the radio with a touch. Barely two feet in front of your car stands . . . Frank.

You climb from the cockpit, out to where the stench of the tires is worse. Even Frank turns toward your car and sniffs the air with a look of disgust on his face.

"Frank! Are you okay?"

You've never seen him like this. A week of beard growth dirties his face. His hair is as wild and unreal as his eyes as they swing to you with shock. Strangest of all, he stands there stark naked, covered in dirt and grime, but naked nonetheless. And his smell . . . my God, it's even worse than the tires.

"Frank, do you need a ride home?"

BRANNNHH! A truck pulls up behind your car and lays on its horn. Frank turns, almost in anger at the interruption.

You take a step toward him. "Come on, buddy. What's wrong?"

BRANHH! BRAH!

Frank ignores it this time and comes toward you. He grabs your shoulders, and in the second most bizarre moment of your life, he sniffs your nose and mouth as you breathe.

"How about we go for a ride?"

BRANNNHHH!

With the fastest motion you've ever seen, Frank locks his lips onto yours in a soft, yet brutal kiss. You feel his tongue flick between your teeth for a second, then vanish.

BRA–

In the back of your mind, you think that even the truck driver is shocked. You also realize that this is definitely

most bizarre moment in your life.

Then it's over. In another flash, Frank is gone, scampering off to the side of the road, disappearing into the trees.

You turn back to your car. Sure enough, the John Deere capped, flannel shirt clad truck driver behind you is frozen with his mandible down and his eyebrows up, both hands white on the steering wheel.

As you climb back into your car, the nothingness returns. The rest of the drive to work, the radio stays off.

"Dana!" you call, jogging across the office toward a tall brunette with ghostly blue eyes. She turns at the sound of your voice and smiles.

"Hi," she returns. "TGIF."

"Definitely," you say as you come to a stop in front of her, even though you can't remember the last time you did anything memorable on a Friday night, much less thanking God for. "Do you know where Frank has been all week?"

"His wife called him in sick."

"Do you know what Frank is working on?"

Her expression changes drastically as if you'd just told her that you killed her cat. Of course, you don't even know if she has a cat. You've exchanged maybe three sentences with the woman since she was hired as the new manager in Frank's department last month. Then she coughs and clears her throat, and her face starts to relax.

"Why do you ask?"

You cock your head sideways, having already planned this bluff. "I can always call Paul and have him ask you. He'll tell me."

Dana returns her winning corporate smile. "Not necessary. He's trying to find a cure for the cold, same as you. It's just that he's working directly with the test subjects. Having his doctorate allows him to do that."

Her bluntness knocks you off guard for a second, but you recover. "Curing the common cold, and then his wife calls him in sick. You know, I've always thought that was pretty–"

"–Ironic! Me, too. I think it's hysterical. I expect him back on Monday. Have a good weekend."

She returns to her original destination, her office, leaving you to watch her walk away. Frank back on Monday? Somehow, you doubt it.

The bells announce your entrance into the Quik Mart to the handful of patrons and an old man behind the register. For your trip today, you grab a pair of TV dinners, two more sodas, and another Snickers bar.

"Mr. Diamond, doesn't your wife usually mind the store on Friday nights?"

"Eh . . ."

BEEP!

"Is she okay?"

BEEP!

You place your hand on the Snickers bar as he reaches for it. "Mr. Diamond."

The man raises his eyes to pierce your heart through your eyes, as if he expects it to be as black as your pupils.

"You want to talk, go use the payphone. Get it?"

He hacks for a moment, then grabs a soda and scans it twice. BEEP! BEEP!

The TV dinners will probably thaw in your trunk and be unsuitable for even your usual meager meal, but that is far less important to you right now than anything else. As you drove here, the zombie was gone, as was the nothingness from your Firebird's interior. You felt alive, with a purpose, and a goal. Something strange is going on, and more important than dinner, or going home to an empty Friday night, you feel a need to *know*.

You ring the doorbell to Frank's house.

A few seconds pass before someone comes to look in the peephole. You take notice of a sigh of relief just before the door opens, and Carolina, Frank's wife, stands within.

"It's good to see you. Please come in."

You enter the house, where you have been a handful of times before. The warmth of the foyer is always inviting, though this time a breath of cold whisks in with you . . . or out through you. Either way, the sensation is the same. A cocker spaniel, Edmund or Edward or something like that, looks to you with hope in his eyes, then turns away, disappointed, and plops down on the ground. A television is on, muted, and a half—empty cup of coffee sits in front of the couch.

Carolina closes the door behind you, and steps past you toward the couch.

"Frank's resting upstairs. I'd rather not wake him because he hasn't been sleeping much lately."

"No, that's okay. I just stopped by to check up on him." You bend at the knees and call to the dog. "Hey, Eddie. Come here, boy."

The dog looks at you from his space on the floor, then to his mother, then sighs.

Carolina forces a half—smile. "Don't worry about him. He hasn't been feeling well lately either. I think he got it from his daddy." She crouchs beside him and scratches behind his ears. "Poor little Edson."

Edson.

She stands again. "Would you like a cup of coffee?"

"That'd be great. Black, please."

She pats the dog as she passes into the kitchen. You sit down in the armchair and notice for the first time what's on TV. The Home Shopping Channel is having a special on wrestling merchandise. As often as Frank mentioned he had an addiction for the male version of a soap opera, he also brought up how much Carolina hated it.

("Yeah, man. I have to set my TV to record it from twelve to two in the morning, then get up two hours early for work on Tuesday so I can watch it. She hates it! Just like the freaks around here. Nobody's man enough to admit wrestling is fun.")

Edson crawls over to you, holding his head low to the ground, as if to apologize for his earlier snubbing. You pet his ears and rub his chin. You are his friend again.

"Frank'll be so upset he missed you," she calls from the kitchen, "But I'm making the decision. You can always come over sometime this weekend."

"Do you think he'll be back in on Monday?"

She reenters the room, a steaming white cup and saucer in her hands. Her eyebrows shift.

"I don't know. He seems to be getting better, but I've thought that before."

"Has he seen a doctor?"

She rolls her eyes. "No. You know Frank. 'If I can't stop a

cold in myself, how can I stop it in the rest of the world.'" She places your coffee on the table in front of you.

You stare at it for a long moment, absently stroking Edson's muzzle. *Thank you* jumps to your lips, but other words make their way out.

"What does he have?"

"Just a cold. A pretty bad one. I'm sure he just needs rest and a lot of fluids." She motions toward the kitchen. "I'm making some chicken soup—"

"I can smell it," you lie, and the look she gives you confirms her lie as well.

Enough games.

"I saw Frank this morning."

Carolina had been reaching for her own coffee, but her arm freezes. Her expression loses its cohesion. She struggles for a moment to maintain it.

"That's . . . not possible. He's been in all day."

"Can I go see him?"

"I told you he's sl—"

"He's not here, Carolina. You don't have to lie to me."

She fights it again, but this time gives up. Her breath sighs out slowly, too calm and forced.

"Where. Where did you see him?"

"On my way to work. On Route 40. He was just standing in the street."

Alarm leaps to her face, but her reaction is still controlled, tame.

"He didn't get hit, did he? Please tell me—"

"No, he didn't. He ran off into the woods." You don't realize how, but you are now sitting with one arm around her. Edson comes over and puts his head on your knee.

"Carolina, when was the last time you saw him?"

"Was he okay? Did he look all right?"

"When he left me, he was safe. Tell me what happened."

She gathers herself, then shakes her head.

"I can't. It wasn't real. It was a dream."

"No. It wasn't. I saw it, too."

She glances at you for a moment, but can't bear your eyes on hers.

"He woke me up early on Sunday. No words. No love. As if someone else was looking through his eyes, someone without a heart."

"What do you mean?"

"Frank never wore clothes when he slept. He preferred if I didn't either."

She pauses, staring into the floor. You stay with her, one arm frozen on her shoulder, the other frozen on Edson's side. He shudders.

"What happened after?"

She says nothing for two deep breaths, lost in the memory of how her life changed forever in an instant. Then she smiles, completely wrong for the words that come from her mouth.

"He left. Without a word. He walked downstairs, and I heard the door close. I was thinking, 'I hope he grabbed his trenchcoat before he went out there naked,' but he didn't. I don't think he took anything."

Her eyes find yours without shame this time. "How was he?"

You stroke her hair, determining the best way to tell her without being cruel and without lying. You exhale strongly.

"He didn't look like himself. Something's happened to him, and I'm going to find out what. I will bring Frank back to you. I promise."

Carolina forces a nod, but you can tell she doesn't believe you. That's fine. You don't really believe yourself.

"Thank you."

She stands from the couch, starts toward the bathroom.

"Is there anything else you need?"

"That old high school composition book? No, he only brought that home a few days a week, and never on Fridays."

The beginning of a plan comes to the forefront of your brain.

Any last bit of nothingness is pushed out. More than anything, you know you cannot go home.

"Actually, yes. Is Frank's log book here?"

"What about his address book?"

She turns, confused.

"Of course. Why?"

"I need to use your phone."

In your ear—the ringing of a phone. In your mind's eye—the phone on the other end of the ring, alone in a dark house, the only light from a dying porch light above the front patio. The cat looks up at the phone for a second, then curls back up and goes to sleep. You know she's not going to be home on a Friday night. Not her. There's no way she's—

Click. "Hello?"

Instantly the image in your mind changes. She's lying on the couch, in a long, flowing silk robe, barely covering her midriff underneath, just relaxing, or waiting for that special someone to call.

"Dana, hi."

"Is this . . . Frank's friend? From work?"

"Yes, it is. I need to talk to you."

"How did you get my number?"

"Frank's address book."

"This isn't a good—"

"We have to talk about Frank. Do you have any plans tonight?"

Her voice raises from bored to intrigued. "No, I don't. I was preparing for a long night of television and chinese food."

TGIF.

"Well, cancel that itinerary. Can you meet me at O'Shea's in an hour?"

"I'll be there."

You hear a muffled cough just before the phone clicks dead

in your ear. Will she actually be there? You hope so, or else answers may be harder to come by.

By the time she walks in, you've already finished one ginger ale and are starting on number two. She sits beside you at the bar and calls the bartender for a Tom Collins.

"You don't drink?" she asks, nodding to your beverage of choice.

"Used to. But when I starting vomiting blood, I decided it would be better not to."

"Good choice," she says, as she takes a sip from her drink. "Now why are we talking about Frank?"

"I need to know exactly where he was in his tests. What was he doing?"

Dana frowns. "That's classified. No one outside of our department and upper management knows the specifics of development and testing."

"Of course. But I have a personal stake in this now." For a moment, her earlier comment stings in your memory. Not finishing your dissertation. How different would things be? You pause longer than you hoped, unsure of how to continue. How about just blurting it out?

"I saw Frank today."

"How is he? Will he be back on Monday?"

"I don't think so."

Without knowing why, you entrust this woman with the truth. Perhaps it's because she's the only one who you think can help you. Perhaps it's because of the promise you made to Carolina. Either way, you tell her everything, from Carolina's account of Sunday morning to your version of what happened on your commute to work. During it all, she sits in silence, not touching her Tom Collins as the ice cubes crackle and melt in her glass. When you are finished, she ignores the straw and swallows a mouthful.

"Do you believe me?"

"How can I not?"

"Thank you."

She doesn't answer, just sits in silence, staring at her glass.

"If you could just . . . I don't know, leave your keys to his office here 'by accident,' so I can get a look at his log book, it wouldn't break the—"

"—Classified clause," she finishes with hopeless smile. "Of course it would. And it wouldn't matter anyway. I've been looking for the book all week. It must be at his house."

"It's not."

"I guess the classified clause doesn't really matter now." She clears her throat, coughs, and begins:

"One of the researchers came up with a theory and had enough proof of it to warrant further investigation. Frank was attached as the tester, due to the quality of his previous work. The researcher had found the cold virus nesting near the front of the cerebrum in several subjects who both did and did *not* have symptoms of the common cold at the time. The single difference between the experimental groups was that the blue lymphocytes of the group without the symptoms were producing enough antibodies to keep the virus in check, while the other group's lymphocytes were not. A few weeks ago, Frank tried injecting more antibodies into the suffering group, but . . . nothing. For some reason, the body rejected anything that was not self-produced in fighting the virus."

She pauses, takes a drink.

"So, at least now you know the source of the common cold."

She shrugs. "In theory. It's up to Frank to prove it." She raises her glass and sets it down again. "*Was* up to Frank. It lies dormant inside of us, waiting for the body to lag in production of its antibody nemesis. Then, it strikes, weakening us until such time as rest and fluids provide the body with enough relief to begin producing again."

She coughs, giving you a moment to ask a question.

"When that failed, what did Frank start on?"

She shakes her head. "I have no idea. For most of the week,

I was occupied with another test that was going well but fell through on Thursday. Frank is supposed to turn in his log book every Friday so I can study it over the weekend, but he slipped out early . . ."

She stops, mouth open. She starts to close her eyes, and a smile comes to her lips.

"Oh, cripes, I hate this."

"What?"

"I have this . . . big sneeze backed up. You know when you have to sneeze and it won't come out? I . . . I hate it.

Wah—choo!

Her head snaps forward with enough force to bring it within millimeters of the table. You smile for a second, but as her face slowly lifts up, much too slowly, you immediately feel something incredibly wrong in the room. Not evil, not dangerous, but wrong.

Her profile is vertical now. Tiny drips of mucus dangle from her nostrils, her eyes stare into what can only be nothingness before her. You recognize the look. One hand reaches up and wipes her nose clean. She whips around on the stool, head cocked back, nose sniffing the air. A look of disgust climbs her tanned cheeks.

"Dana, please don't do this."

She turns to you, sniffing the air around you. She smiles. A man walks by with a cigar in his mouth, and as the smoke blows into your faces, she jumps from the stool in anger and fear, pushes the man to the ground, and bursts outside through the front door.

Part of you tries to hesitate, to let it go. Someone else will get her, someone else will find her, won't they? But your body won't let you. You follow through the door, and as the wind hits you square in the face, you remember Frank . . . and run.

You've been following her for an hour. Her footspeed is incredible, inhuman. Several times she's lost you, but with good instincts or blind luck you've always found her again. She stops sometimes, raising her nose to the air, and the smells of industry seem to frighten her, while the smells of the forest call her. Yet time and time again she is drawn curiously to her fear, sliding down an alley, rubbing her hands over the glass doors of a Quik Mart, or caressing an oil stain on the rugged asphalt of a parking lot.

And now she stands, with fear all around her, the safety of the nothingness nowhere to be found. Manmade life surrounds her. You call to her, but she cannot hear over the cacophony of engines and horns that create the black hole your voice falls into. Yet still you shout:

"Dana! Get out of there! You have to move!"

The loudest silence in the known world comes from your lips, swallowed by some relative of the nothingness. The night, blacker than death, is her enemy. Below her feet, a spotted white line. On one side, a convertible flies by, dodging her at the last instant. On the other side, a minivan slams on its brakes but still does not come to a halt until it is twenty feet past her. The driver yells something from his window, but you can hear that no more than you can speak to the thing that was once a woman only ten feet away.

Her eyes flutter; her balance shifts. Dana leans in your direction . . . takes two steps toward you to regain her balance.

A lone horn cries into the night . . .

"The driver tried to stop," you'll tell police later. Watching that happen, in the horrifying slow motion in which such things always do, it's the most horrifying moment of your life. But later, when you wake up in the middle of the night to the sound of your own coughing, it's even worse.

It's 3:00 a.m.

Nothingness is back. You had thought it vanquished, but sitting alone at home after Dana's death, it wrapped itself around you like an old lover and whispered into your ear . . . *sleep.* Your enemy It gave you no choice but to absorb it, accept it, and let it imbue your being with calmness. Because of it, you feel in control of yourself and the world as your tires blaze a trail to your office.

". . . yet another pedestrian casualty on the Crosstown Freeway last night. The woman's family has just given us permission to reveal the victim's name. Dana—"

Victim of your hand, the radio dies. Why were you listening to it? Why have you *ever* listened to it? God, will nothing make sense anymore?

Kahf.

Kahf. Kahf.

Frank's lab is the epitome of organization. His desk is spotless, his coffee cup sparking clean. No sign of his lab book, but you've just begun looking.

A row of rat cages lines one wall, and the captives bounce off the walls in feeble attempts to escape. Since you're here earlier than the attendant who will feed them, you take the responsibility upon yourself. Strangely though, no rat touches their food while you are near. Frank told you once that he had "practically tamed each and every one of them," so that they enjoyed human company and took comfort in the act of eating or playing in front of them. Were these those very same rats, who glare in fear at your unclipped fingernails dropping food into their dishes?

You veer away from the bottles and beakers and chemicals that make up the lab proper. No sense messing with any of that until you have uncovered the log book and can pick up where Frank left off.

You wipe a slightly runny nose. The desk is locked, but thanks to Dana's purse, left intact at the bar, you have that key, and it opens with ease. Inside are a scattered assortment of pens and pencils, a ruler, copies of *Milstein's Biology* and *Compounds and Moles: The Definitive Chemical Research Compendium Vol. 1*, and a stack of wrestling magazines. Wrestling. You remember what he said about wrestling and the people at the company. Would Dana really have been so short-sighted?

You lift the top magazine, with a picture of the current champ on it. Below it lies another superstar, then the tag champs with the belts. Below that, a magazine with the female valets on the cover will not budge, as if it is glued to the bottom of the desk. Carefully, you pry it up. Sure enough, a hollowed out bottom reveals it black and white spotted treasure.

Page One:

Thursday, January 12, 4:15PM (cont'd)–Isolations of the supposed "cold virus" have proven to be impossible through Dr. Wengall's testing. I disagree with his theories in principle because isolating the viral bacteria in a clean environment to test its reactions will prove NOTHING in regards to how it will react in its natural environment of the human body. For his sake, I wish Dr. Wengall the worst of luck. Should his tests prove successful but useless in a valid environment, he's going to get fired. No doubt about it. How this affects my work is yet to be seen, though if his tests are successful, I can look forward to a few months of wasting my time trying to duplicate it.

Slowly, the memories return. Nine years of post-graduate work leading to an unfinished dissertation that still sits in your beaten-up gray backpack return to the sponge in your skull as Frank's notes take over your thoughts. Pages fly by, things begin to make sense, but the nothingness tells you that your true enemy slides away with the sweeping hand of the schoolhouse clock.

Friday, October 13, 12:30PM–Well, I will definitely need to hide this beginning today, though I thought I might be able to fake my way through another week. Dana has been blessedly ab-

sent, leaving me to pursue this cure on my own, out from under her pathetically inexperienced watchful eye. However, all of this still needs to be recorded for myself. Beta FD has progressed through all tests successfully. Beta FD is a manmade virus that enters the cerebrum of the life form when not suffering the symptoms of a cold and creates antibodies using the body's own blue lympho-cytes to kill the latent cold virus. Tonight, I will return after all have gone home to test Beta FD on my favorite rat, Red. I'm sure he'll thank me for it.

Friday, October 13, 11:30PM–Success! For the most part. Two hours after injecting Beta FD into Red, his EEG2 shows a noticeable decrease in the size of the virus, and the body is accept-ing the alien virus' antibodies as its own! Since the virus itself is self-destructive, I expect his brain to be clear by tomorrow night. Oddly though, he seems to be suffering from severe cold symptoms, though I suspect that is the virus's last ditch effort of self-salvation and should disappear with the virus itself.

Saturday, October 14, 10:30PM–The virus has disappeared from Red completely, and the virus created by Beta FD has van-ished as well. I wish I could be more excited though. The cold is gone, true, as I expected, but Red seems to have forgotten his training and has reverted to his natural wild tendencies. He has tried to escape his cage and hurt himself in the process. Even stranger though, is that the other rats have followed suit . All of them have turned on their training and become as wild as the wolf. I can only hope that this is a temporary side effect that will go away in time.

As a side note, I believe I must have caught Red's cold (laugh) as I woke this morning to a sore throat and a hesitant cough. (Sigh.) Like son, like father.

You look up from the last page of Frank's book and cough.

Some of it makes sense and some of it doesn't. You must read some more. There must be other notes around here.

Kahf. Kahf.

Deduction. Frank would have been proud of you for using that. For hours you have searched for anything, notes, scraps of paper, a half-labeled beaker, but nothing has provided you with answers. But now you've come up with one on your own. If Beta FD produces a virus that is designed to destroy itself eventually, couldn't it still reproduce and spread through the air like a normal virus before self-destructing? The coughing. It begins to make sense. All of it, except for the reversion to an animal-like human that Frank and Red and Dana and presumably the others all went through. It must all be somehow connected. First things first. You have to find a way to kill the Beta virus before it can continue to spread. And you have to hurry. It's getting late.

Cerebrum. Something sticks in the back of your mind about that, about what Dana said. Isn't there a dictionary around here somewhere?

ce•re•brum \se—"re—brem, "ser—e—brem\ noun [L] (1615): an enlarged anterior or upper part of the brain; esp : the expanded anterior portion of the brain that in higher mammals overlies the rest of the brain, consists of cerebral hemispheres and connecting structures, and is considered to be the seat of conscious mental processes : telencephalon

Conscious mental processes . . .
"Excuse me?"
The voice sends you into a spin; the dictionary falls to the floor. Behind you, the nighttime security guard stands with one hand balanced over his holstered shock-baton.
"I'm going to need to see your badge, please."

You force your heart to calm down, reach into your pocket, and produce your badge.

"You scared the heck out of me."

The guard merely raises an eyebrow as he checks your ID against a computer on his wrist. You see a green light flash, and the man smiles.

"Sorry about that. Just didn't see you come in."

"I got here this morning, around eleven."

The guard elevates the eyebrow again. "Well, I hope you'll be heading on home soon. It's after midnight, you know."

He cocks his head a little and looks at you curiously. "Are you feeling all right?"

You nod. "Yes, thank you. I feel fine."

The guard smiles and whistles his way from the room. He probably whistled his way in, but you were too focused to hear him. After midnight? You haven't left the lab all day. Either your body functions have slowed down, or time has sped up. Regardless, you must get back to work. Your third attempt at an anti-Beta virus is just starting to boil, something the first two were not able to do. The tiny bubbles over the creamy yellow liquid are the first positive sign you've had all night. Of course, given how many years it's been since you were in a lab doing work, the fact that you haven't blown up the lab is considered a positive sign.

As the glass beaker shatters before you, it seems like a dream. It can't be real. Part of your mind sees it kind of fuzzy, like it happened long ago, in another lifetime, and another part of your mind sees it for the dangerous reality that it is . . . pieces of glass that can slice the life out of you in an instant. The greenish substance from the inside splashes around the lab, on you, on Frank's notes, and all over the sinks. For a second, your thought is to clean it up, but that thought vanishes as another pushes its way to the surface. Something is building deep inside you, a tension, a stress, a push . . . something that feels and breathes like an animal that wants to be released, something with more power and control than the nothingness ever had. Off in the distance, you hear another beaker shatter, and somewhere, the recesses of your mind tell you that your arms are swinging wildly. But you can't tell because your eyes are closed, your head is spasming, and your nose is about to explode. As much as you want to fight it, relief can't come quickly enough.

You sneeze.

Sterling Silver

by Scott Braden

From the safety of his top-secret headquarters housed deep within the earth, Scott Braden has spent more than half of his lifetime examining heroes (as well as the concept of heroism itself) in his various writings—an obsession that began when he took crayon in hand and scribbled out his first play, "The Blue Bandit Had a Change of Heart," at the tender age of six.

Having grown up to become a professional writer (he writes stuff, people pay him), as well as an enthusiast of classic pulp magazines and the four-color medium of comics, the now 31-year-old has cranked out a wealth of articles for newspapers, magazines, and trade publications—as well as a single comic book tale entitled "Favorite Son" that, gosh darn it, he's really proud of.

To this day, Braden delights in studying the motivations behind ordinary individuals (both fictional and flesh-and-blood) who become extraordinary by answering "the call," rising to "the challenge," and fighting "the good fight." He also confesses to being intrigued with the repercussions these heroes might face for their acts of bravery and their sense of justice , as can be seen in his quietly apocalyptic tale, "Sterling Silver."

Sterling Silver

The road ahead of Reid was swallowed in unending darkness. Shining brightly, his roadster's headlights pierced the highway before him like silver bullets.

This realization brought a small smile to Reid's lips. In all his many years, he had never once succumbed to the night. Of course, he had never felt comfortable riding on anything without four legs either, which is why he was so absorbed with the shadowy road ahead.

Until very recently, looking ahead had always been his way. To him, the past had been nothing but a lonesome stranger best forgotten. But now that he was so close to his destination, he couldn't help but look back at his life.

Although Reid had been out of the public eye for decades, those who still recognized him knew his journey had been a very long one. He was well aware that he was an old man. Hell, he would be the first to admit it. He was tired, dog-tired even, but the journey wasn't about him. No matter what some folks might have said, it never had been. Still, for all the good he had done, he had lost too many friends along the way, and seen too many good men die upon life's winding path. He had witnessed first hand the evil that men do, and immediately recognized it for what it was: a disease. For all his works, after all these many years, he finally realized he was helpless to prevent it from spreading—and that no cure was within his reach.

Or so he thought.

The world had become a nightmare. Reid felt in his heart of hearts that only he had the power to set it right somehow. Thus, the lonesome journey beckoned him once more—like it had in all those years before.

Reid searched the sky for a glimpse of the moon and stars. As a young man, he had ridden across this magnificent land on his noble steed, under a starlit sky. Although it sounded a bit cliché, the night sky comforted him during desperate times.

He glanced up at the empty blackness and sighed deeply. The desert air filled his lungs with ice—but what lay immediately ahead of him chilled him to the bone.

"Merciful Jesus . . . !"

Reid quickly slammed on the brakes, barely preventing the roadster from hitting what appeared to be a group of people, lying face down and scattered across the road.

His mind going a mile a minute, he slowed it long enough to correct himself. Not people . . . corpses.

Shaking, he slowly calmed himself and got out of the car. By the smell and the state of their bodies, it appeared that they had been dead for days. Murdered, or rather butchered, by the looks of it. He'd seen similar ways of dying too many times before.

As if on cue, he became the hero. Perhaps he could deduce what had killed them, maybe even avenge their deaths in some small way. In his younger years, he had been quite a detective—although he needn't know the first thing about criminology to ascertain that it had been a family that now lay cold and lifeless on the road.

Reason began to take control of him again. He was still an old man, and there was nothing he could do. Although, someone ought to bury them, he thought. It was the only decent thing to do.

Then, as if somebody had grabbed him by the shoulder, he stopped. He couldn't expend his energy on this—he had to conserve his strength for that which lay ahead of him. The place where this journey into mystery would lead him.

Settling back into his seat, Reid crossed himself—saying a prayer for these, the latest victims of the Madness.

Starting the engine of his car, he realized that his journey, *this journey*, now felt more necessary than ever.

Although born in a much simpler time, Reid was no stranger to madness and mayhem. His parents, who traveled from the streets of Dublin to this great nation in search of a better life, familiarized him as to the Devil's ways—educating him on the Wicked One's grasp over man and the world. As he grew to become a man himself—a lawman, in fact—he soon discovered that Ol' Scratch had little or nothing to do with the evil in men's souls.

They were quite capable of achieving that all by themselves.

To that end, it was Reid's view that most men were drawn to wickedness and evil, and willfully spread it to others. This outbreak would continue until someone stood up to fight it. Someone like himself.

As a lawman, he began the fight, but soon realized that a badge and a gun could only do so much against the criminal element. It was then he traded in symbols of justice to *become* a symbol of justice, and with the aid of a like-minded partner, set out to tame the West.

As time went on, his brother-at-arms grew old and passed on, leaving him to carry on the fight alone in a larger, more uncertain world. Over the years, Reid would expand his struggle against injustice across nations. He rode with Teddy Roosevelt in the Spanish-American War. He fought against the Hun in World War I. He fought for the Allies in World War II. And then finally, he had no more fight left in him.

During the late '50s and early '60s, he watched the world change. Dramatically. He watched as the morals and values that he had fought for suddenly came into question. He watched as mankind expanded its dominion into space. He watched as men he thought he could trust, who stood up for what he was led to believe was right, became seen for what they really were: liars and lunatics.

It was all too much for him, and he did what he had never done before. He ran away.

He went east.

Years rolled by, and he continued to live a menial, day-to-day existence. He became a lone stranger in an even stranger land, watching in horror as riots decimated cities, police terrorized those they swore to protect, and death and despair became the status quo.

It was during this time that Reid felt the Madness had begun—our slow, steady decent into Hell. At first, he ignored the signs. For a while, a very long while, he even lied to himself, saying that things would get better.

It was during this period of denial that the dreams began. Dreams of great cities sinking into lost seas, of entire villages mysteriously disappearing into the night, of a great man dying for the sins of others. These were dreams of sacrifice and ending, dreams that brought an old man on a great journey of faith and hope.

Dreams that led Reid back west, to seek out the source of the Madness. A journey that, according to the feeling in his gut, has almost reached its end.

Driving on, the old man took off his white hat, and stroked his weathered hands through his thick, silver hair. For all his grumbling, even he had to admit that he looked good for his age . . . however old that may be.

Truth be told, he had stopped counting birthdays a long ways back.

Catching light in his peripheral vision, Reid glimpsed up at a gas station sign.

"It's one of those new-fangled automated ones," he muttered under his breath. He hated those goddamn things. Although a loner by nature, he preferred the company of people to that of machines.

Reid never took too kindly to machines. The condition of his roadster was evidence of this.

Finally, in a moment of clarity, reason prevailed and he began to curse his stubbornness. It was the Irish in him. Still, he needed gas, there was a gas station, and that was that.

Driving into the station, Reid found himself joining its only other occupants: a young couple and their hot-rod car. It looked like something out of the old pulp magazines he and his partner would glance at occasionally, between adventures. Resembling a strange metallic bug, only sleeker, the car carried two passengers—a young man, who was pumping gas, and a dark, exotic-looking woman, who was seated in the vehicle.

Reid drove up to the fuel pump. Having tried to read the nearly impenetrable instructions, he began to shake his head.

"Do you need help, sir?" asked the young man, politely.

"I thought you would never ask, young man," said Reid, smiling. "Thank you, kindly."

Reid looked the boy over. He appeared as if he had recently been beaten. Badly.

"I hope you don't mind me asking," said the boy, "but are you an actor? I feel as if I've seen you somewhere before . . ."

Reid thought of Rogers, the singing cowboy who had his beloved horse stuffed. He never understood the reasoning behind that. It seemed blasphemous somehow. Then, there was that Moore fellow . . .

"An actor?" said the old man, smiling. "Me? No, I was never an actor. Sure, I've met more than my share of actors over the years, but no, I was never one myself. I was a lawman in my younger days."

"You were a cop?" the boy asked, his demeanor suddenly changing from friendly to threatening. "I would never have taken you for a pig!"

Reid was taken aback by the young man's response: "Now

hold on there, son. Where I come from, men who fought on the side of the law were to be respected and admired."

"Open your eyes, old man! People have died because of 'lawmen' like you. The laws that you and your kind enforce are enslaving us one man at a time. The cities have become ghettos, with police as executioners, and our leaders as tyrants. That's why my girlfriend and I are heading east—we're leaving this hell behind us!"

As the boy spoke, Reid thought of the Madness. He then looked over at the frightened young girl in the car. She was far too young to be running from her home. They both were.

Seeing the young couple, Reid remembered a young Indian woman from his past. The curves of her body, the warmth of her embrace, the way she moved underneath him—these were moments in time that would never leave him. To this day, the memories continued to ebb and flow within him like a great river. As of late, he often found himself submerged in her memory, all the while damning himself for what he left behind in the name of a greater cause.

A cause that, if he were to believe the boy, was apparently lost.

Reid shook off his doubts. Whether he was blessed with pure determination or cursed with sheer stubbornness, one thing was for certain: he wasn't one to give up. Not again.

"Back in my time, lawmen fought those kinds of injustices," he quietly countered. "Some of us still do."

The boy began to laugh. Then, as quickly as he started, he stopped.

Reid aimed his solemn blue eyes at the boy's. "Don't you believe in heroes anymore, son," he asked in earnest.

"You're serious, aren't you?" the boy said, tears welling up in his eyes. "You really think that there are heroes left believing in, don't you, old man?"

Reid paused. "With all my heart, son. That's why I'm here . . . to set it all right again."

Reid could tell that the boy was struggling to believe him.

"You and your young lady friend make your way back home, son. Things should be right by the time you arrive."

"But how . . . ?"

Reid put his hand on the boy's shoulder. "I can't explain how, but that's why I'm here. To set things right once and for all."

"I know you . . ." the boy said with widening eyes.

Reid shook the boy's hand. A smile materialized across his face.

"Never forget, son."

Opening the door to his car, Reid stopped to tip his hat to the young lady. "Nice to meet you, m'am. Thank you both for your kind assistance." And with that, he drove away.

Reid looked back—watching the boy stammer, barely managing to wander over to his car.

He imagined the girl looking on, asking: "Who was that old man?"

With that, he continued to drive on in his silver roadster—turning his back from the approaching dawn.

Reid couldn't stop thinking about what the boy had said: "You really think there are heroes left believing in, don't you, old man?"

What if the boy was right? What if, in this day and age, believing in heroes was a luxury that no one–including himself—could afford?

Suddenly, Reid noticed a dense fog began to form around the car. Glancing at the rearview mirror, Reid lost sight of the rising sun. At the same time, an invisible hand gripped his heart.

His world began spinning out of control.

He began to lose his bearings.

He began to grow cold and numb.

"It's not time yet . . ." he angrily muttered through clenched teeth. "I've come so far . . ."

Clutching the steering wheel, Reid fought to get control of

his body again—just as a gray figure appeared before him on the road. Summoning what strength he had left, he slammed on the brake pedal, collapsing in the process.

As he sank away into oblivion, Reid cursed the darkness, which had at long last overtaken him.

Opening his eyes, Reid found himself outside the roadster, lying on the ground. Standing above him was a towering grayish figure. As his clarity of vision returned, he noticed that the figure was that of a man. Looking ancient and powerful, the Gray Man stood well over seven-feet tall, sported tattered clothes and hat, and wore a black cloth patch over his right eye. Above the stranger circled two black ravens—scavenger birds that Reid first imagined were buzzards.

"You insult my pets by referring to them as mere vultures, boy," warned the Gray Man. "That is not wise."

"How did you . . . ?"

"I'm more than I seem, boy," answered the Gray Man with a smile. "As are you."

Reid looked around him. Scattered about were bodies of men, of different races and, apparently, of different eras. At closer inspection, he found that some were wearing animal skins while others were dressed in brightly colored clothing.

"Where am I?" asked Reid. "Am I dead?"

"No, boy, you're not dead . . . yet," the Gray Man chuckled. "Soon, though, you may wish you were."

The Gray Man waved his hand and signaled for Reid to look all around him. On the ground, there were more corpses.

Reid scanned his grim surroundings—eventually having to close his eyes. He had had his fill of looking at the dead today.

After a long pause, he finally asked, "Who are they?"

"They were heroes all," said the Gray Man. "Look, over there: the barbarian king from an age long vanished. He had a great fire burning within him, he did. Over there is the pale rider with the sword as black as the night itself—even blacker than my ravens. It had been said that the rider's sword would not only steal the life of its victims, but their very souls. Then there's the mild-mannered man-god in his colorful garb . . . the demonic man from a land far to the east . . .

Listening to the Gray Man's strange words, Reid began to get up, intent on making his way back to the roadster. That's where the guns are, he thought to himself. That's how I'll escape.

"You are much like them, Reid. Why do you look surprised? Because I know your name, is that it? I know everything about you, boy. For you see, you are my ward, like all these warriors were."

"Who are you," Reid asked.

"I have many names, boy," said the gray figure. "Men have called me the Gray Man, the King of the Highways, the Chooser of the Slain, the All-Father. I'm all these things and more. Right now, though, I am your guide. Through me, you will 'set the world right' . . . that's how you refer to your destiny, is it not?"

"How do I do this?" Reid answered, almost pleading. "How do I succeed where all these brave men have failed?"

"Because of what's around you. This is your place of power. All of these fallen warriors were brave and strong, but they were also foreign to this land. You, on the other hand, are more than just its defender; you are its essence, its spirit. This place guides you and empowers you and gives you the strength to meet the next day. Haven't you wondered how you have been able to live as long as you have? You . . . a mere mortal?"

Reid stood silent.

"The darkness before you, this unending night, this 'Madness' you seek, it is all the evil that exists within the world. It is all of man's sins given form. It needs to be cleansed by one who is good and pure. Tell me, Reid . . . are you that man?"

Having finally reached his roadster, he looked at the two six-guns in his hands and then at the Gray Man himself.

Once again, Reid became the hero.

"Tell me what I need to do."

With his black mask and his silver bullets, Reid would ride in and save the day. At least, that's what they used to say about him in days of yesteryear—the pulp writers and the radio players with their stories.

Closing his eyes, he imagined that somewhere in another place and time, he was with his Indian love, enjoying morning's first light. In this dream of his, he was happier than he had ever been before, than he ever could be.

It was a good dream, but then again, he had led a good life.

He thought of his old friend—a blood brother who he had shared many adventures with. He thought of all of the many people he helped, the lives he saved.

With that, he put on his mask and his white hat. Pulling his guns from their holsters, Reid whispered a silent prayer, and focused on the darkness ahead—aiming his six shooters straight into the abyss.

He couldn't explain it, but suddenly he felt younger and stronger than he had in years. He pulled back on the guns' hammers until they clicked into position, and then he smiled his ranger's grin.

It *was* his time to set things right.

Like a man possessed, he began to shoot the hell out of the darkness—his guns blazing brightly into the great, wide forever. Within the gunsmoke and chaos, he glimpsed his Valhalla and his lonesome journey's end.

It shone before him like sterling silver.